PRAISE FOR

The Second Season

"Women with ambition, especially in sports, are often told: 'Be quiet. Shrink. Don't dream too big.' Emily Adrian's *The Second Season* squashes any notion of that. It shines in its portrayal of a woman protagonist who will not dim her light. This book is brilliant, engrossing and should be read by every person, basketball fan or not. My only wish is that Adrian had written this when I was a young girl, because it would have made me feel seen, encouraged, and understood."

—MIRIN FADER, staff writer for
The Ringer and author of *Giannis: The Improbable Rise of an NBA MVP*

"In Emily Adrian's hands, the most exciting story during the NBA Finals is not on the court, but on the sidelines. This book will draw you in right away and you won't put it down until you've read the final sentence."

—TOM MCALLISTER, author of *How to Be Safe*

"To borrow a sports idiom, Emily Adrian really stuffs the stat sheet here. She writes as engagingly and insightfully about basketball and broadcasting as she does about work, love, friendship, ambition, motherhood, aging, and the power and frailty of the body. Smart, tough, passionate Ruth Devon is a winning protagonist, and her poignant story is both suspenseful and meditative. *The Second Season* is a terrific sports novel, yes, but it's also just a terrific novel."

—CHRIS BACHELDER, author of *The Throwback Special*

"You don't have to love basketball or care about motherhood to love this book, but this book will make you fall in love with both."

—RUFI THORPE, author of *The Knockout Queen*

"Sport and bodies and ambition, motherhood and womanhood and obsession: Emily Adrian's *The Second Season* masterfully gets you inside the particular thrill of sport whether it was ever capable of thrilling you before, and, deftly and warmly, pulls off the extraordinary feat of forcing you to root for a complicated, unapologetically ambitious fortysomething woman who also happens to be a mom. I loved this novel for its alacrity and its humanity and its humor, its attention to the body, and its willingness to let its characters pursue impossible-seeming dreams."

—LYNN STEGER STRONG, author of *Want*

The Second Season

EMILY ADRIAN

The Second Season

A Novel

BLACK STONE
PUBLISHING

Copyright © 2021 by Emily Adrian
Published in 2021 by Blackstone Publishing
Cover and book design by Alenka Vdovič Linaschke

The characters and events in this book are fictitious.
Any similarity to real persons, living or dead, is coincidental
and not intended by the author.

Printed in the United States of America

First edition: 2021
ISBN 978-1-7999-3214-7
Fiction / Women

1 3 5 7 9 10 8 6 4 2

CIP data for this book is available
from the Library of Congress

Blackstone Publishing
31 Mistletoe Rd.
Ashland, OR 97520

www.BlackstonePublishing.com

For Wes, forever

CHAPTER ONE

Ruth's daughter fell, as children do, in slow motion.

The baby had climbed up on her father's weight bench and was pumping her legs back and forth as if to propel a swing at the playground. Ruth was supervising. She was also searching the garage for a particular set of eight-pound free weights, intent on working out during Ariana's morning nap. Ruth threw a glance over her shoulder just as the baby leaned forward to admire her pink sneakers in action. Perched closer to the edge of the bench than Ruth had realized, the baby wobbled. Ruth lunged, expecting Ariana to regain her balance and underestimating her daughter's commitment to the sippy cup clenched in her hands. Ari toppled. Her head hit the concrete first; the rest of her somersaulted with a sickening series of thuds.

It was the ensuing silence, the absence of cries, that took Ruth's breath away.

In the days, weeks, and years that followed, she replayed the incident in her mind until she lost the memory to the murky currents of guilt and anxiety and fear. For how long was Ariana quiet? Was she crying by the time Ruth scooped her into her arms, or did she release her first scream as Ruth, with a new mother's panic, lurched into the kitchen and dialed 911? The baby's blood, Ruth could have sworn, was a more vibrant red than her own had ever been—and there was so much of it! She couldn't tell if the origin was Ariana's mouth, nose, or a gash near the goose egg swelling fast on her forehead. Did the blood really mat the baby's eyelashes, coat her teeth, and soak through Ruth's shirt to the beige panels of the nursing bra she was still wearing, months after weaning? Did Ruth press an ice pack to the bump? Did she call Lester and ask him to meet her at the hospital—or did she stand in place, hold her child, and sob?

The minutes before the fall are what Ruth remembers clearly. She can still conjure the desperation with which she worked to uncover the free weights from the tidal wave of sporting equipment that had swallowed the garage in the late nineties. They were hoarding the evidence of their preparenthood pastimes: golf clubs, tennis rackets, baseball mitts, ice skates, and balls for six or seven different sports, any one of which could reduce her and Lester to hot-cheeked rivals. She hadn't laid a finger on any of it in sixteen months, and now that Ariana was sleeping through the night Ruth was eager to get back into shape. She still believed in her shape. That her adolescent frame was waiting, unscathed, beneath a shedable layer of maternal flab. All she needed was forty-five minutes, preferably an hour, long enough to get her heart pounding on the treadmill. To curl the weights toward her chest, reacquaint her body with the sensation of resistance.

Ariana's head had hit a crack in the cement, which tore open the flesh near her fuzzy hairline. She needed three stitches. She needed a hit of nitrous oxide to endure the suturing and another to tolerate the invasions of the pediatric dentist, who admitted there was nothing to do but wait for her adult teeth to fill in the gaps. Ruth wept when she realized her daughter's top incisors were missing and again, later, when she could not find them among the blood on the garage floor. If the baby's teeth were not in her mouth, Ruth wanted to secret them in a drawer as her own mother had done.

At home, they set Ariana up with a tape of *Dumbo*. Too young to say elephant, she was old enough to wave her arm in front of her face like a trunk. She fell asleep on the couch still holding a half-drunk bottle of milk to her lips, the nipple resting against her traumatized gums.

Ruth's fingertips hovered over the bandage. She said to Lester, "That's going to scar."

Lester shrugged. "So she won't be a model." It was a safe bet that, against all odds, they lost.

The phone rang in the kitchen. The phone was attached to the wall by the kind of corkscrew cord teenage girls used to twirl between their fingers. Lester got up to answer it. His casual "Hey, man" could have been addressed to anyone.

In the doorway, Ruth's husband turned and locked eyes with her. In her memory his face blanches, as if he comprehends the call's full significance—the life about to unfurl from it. Hers.

"Just a sec. Let me talk to her." He cupped a hand over the receiver. His contrived neutrality made Ruth's hair follicles tense. "It's Benny Hoss. One of the announcers dropped out. Family emergency."

Hoss was the athletic director at Georgetown.

"I can tell him we're in the middle of one ourselves," Lester said.

"In the middle of what?"

"A family emergency."

Ruth's hand was buried in Ariana's curls. On the screen,

Dumbo's mother was in shackles, locked inside the truck for mad elephants. Thank God Ariana was already asleep; the film was darker than either Ruth or Lester had remembered.

"Don't tell him that," Ruth said.

By most measures, the game was not important: Georgetown versus Oklahoma, the first round of an early-season tournament that would be largely forgotten by Selection Sunday. But it was Georgetown, Ruth's alma mater. The game would be broadcast on a cable channel. If Ruth wanted the job she had ninety minutes to get herself to DC and to the new MCI Center. A goal that I-66 could easily grant or deny.

Lester had been Ruth's coach in college. Now, as they stared impassively at each other, she willed him to become her coach again. *Tell me I can do this,* she thought. *Tell me I have to. That I won't choke.* But Lester remained her husband. A father worried about his daughter—or else worried about putting the baby to bed by himself. Where were the extra-absorbent diapers for sleepy time? Where was the beloved board book about hippos throwing a house party? What should he do if she cried out in the night?

For the first quarter of Ariana's first year, Ruth had never slept more than two hours at a time. The baby's cries woke her constantly, and before her brain could assign a source to the sound it conjured another kind of chaos. The infant stirred, and Ruth heard Nikes squeaking against a waxed floor; she wailed, and Ruth heard the buzzer as the ball left her hands.

"Tell him I'll do it," she said, scrambling from the couch, letting Ariana flop to her side on the cushions.

As a player, Ruth's career had ended in college. It was her senior season, a tough-luck landing that exploded her knee and left her writhing on the floor. (Even now, if an urge to laugh threatens an interview, she need only think of that *pop*, the sobering sound of her ligament rupturing.) The formation of the WNBA was still a few years off. Had Ruth known it was coming, she might have let them operate. The thing was, no surgeon could promise a full reconstruction would restore her talent. The other thing was, at least half her heart was already devoted to Lester and to the brown-eyed, bow-legged babies they would cook up together.

Throughout the Big East, Ruth had been known as "that bitch from the District." On the court she gave herself over to a delicious, guiltless aggression. She scratched and she clawed. She tripped and she hip-checked. When the refs weren't looking she grabbed freely at jerseys and, once, at a rival's preposterous pigtails. If a shorter girl dared defend her in the post, Ruth did nothing to prevent a sharp elbow from colliding with flimsy cartilage. Was the violence incongruous with her desire to be a stay-at-home mom? Ruth didn't think so; Dumbo's mother beat the shit out of those circus-going bullies teasing her baby for his oversized ears. Basketball and motherhood had something in common: each required your animal self.

Young enough to believe she had made a choice, Ruth graduated and married Lester. The scandal of their marriage was mitigated by Lester receiving a well-timed offer: that same summer, he left Georgetown to become the assistant coach of the men's team at American University. Eight minutes by car, yet worlds removed from Ruth and her reputation. Few of her husband's new colleagues sustained any interest in the girls' half of the NCAA. Ruth got pregnant and gave birth—precipitous labor, cinematic, she could take it—and sank into ruinous, mammalian love. She did her best to confine her basketball addiction to her alma mater's radio station, whose producers let her call women's games from the nosebleeds. Her audience was notional. Ruth liked to imagine former teammates swaying with colicky infants, listening for the score. For those games she did both play-by-play and color; she told you when a girl got a shot up, as well as the girl's major, hometown, skill set, and career aspirations.

Television had not been Ruth's goal. The red light of the camera held no appeal. Though the consensus was that she signed up for a certain amount of scrutiny, Ruth never anticipated the mob of men analyzing her hair, legs, glasses, voice, the shadows beneath her eyes, the way she stood, the way she gripped the microphone. What she wanted was to be there. On the floor, close enough to see the sweat beading, to feel the reverberations of the rim. Georgetown's team that year included sophomore Jeremy Baines, a kid whose ability to dunk after a single dribble from half-court left announcers braying in shock. He would be drafted in June, maybe first overall. Ruth *needed* to be there. She was twenty-five—already someone's wife and someone's mom—and desperate for permission to care about the game as much as she did.

She owned a single wine-colored blazer that she pulled over a vaguely catholic blouse. (Lester said, "Don't wear that," and Ruth vowed never to take it off.) These choices would come back to haunt her ten years later, in a video uploaded to YouTube by a Ruth Devon fan account, the audio and picture slightly out of sync. Ruth's middle-school-age daughter would watch the opener muttering *no-no-no* beneath her breath and, from that day forward, forbid her mother from appearing on camera in any outfit she had not personally approved. For now, Ariana remained a toddler passed out on the couch. Ruth remained green enough to assume men would take a woman announcer more seriously if she looked plain, unattractive. She should have asked a man.

Or a woman.

Smooth sailing on 66. Ruth's palms slipped against the steering wheel. How could she call a game when she'd never watched the team practice, never interviewed its coaches? Georgetown's record last year was twenty-four and six—or it was twenty-six and four. Baines was a preseason all-American, but who were the less-heralded freshmen? Ruth had once known, since forgotten. And now she was paying to park in a lot near the stadium, having received no other instructions. She was filming the opener on the sideline, spooked in the glare of the red light. Her co-announcer elbowed her; she was looking in the wrong direction. Finally, Ruth was pulled to the analyst's chair. Pep band. Tip-off. Engrossed in the action between the lines, Ruth resumed knowing everything. She would never remember what she said, only that her commentary filled the gaps in the play-by-play. She could have been watching at home, chattering to Lester through a mouthful of popcorn. It was that effortless.

Late in the first half, Jeremy Baines came down hard on his ankle, his foot sideways underneath. For the second time that day, Ruth drew a sharp blast of air into her lungs. Jeremy recovered; he came back after halftime, and GU trimmed a nine-point deficit to one. With twenty seconds on the clock Baines was alone with the ball at the top of the key, waiting to be reborn. It was November; the madness was scheduled for March. But when Jeremy Baines hit a fadeaway at the buzzer, fifteen thousand people in Washington, DC forgot the month, the year, and their mothers' maiden names.

"My goodness," was all Ruth needed to say.

Jeremy Baines prostrated himself on the court like he'd won a national championship. His teammates piled on top of him. The Oklahoma players stood with hands on hips; and was their point guard crying? Something Ruth still misses about college basketball is how volatile, how prone to tears they all are.

At home, well past midnight, she pulled the minivan into the garage and heard something plastic crunch beneath her tires. Instantly she remembered Ariana's sippy cup flying from her hands, the startled O of her lips as she fell forward, frightened but certain her mother would catch her. Ruth would throw herself between the concrete floor and her daughter's soft, new body. She would absorb the contact, cushion the blow, knock her own teeth out if she had to.

What choice did she have?

CHAPTER TWO

SEVENTEEN YEARS LATER

The night before Game One of the NBA finals, Ruth paces the floor of her Seattle hotel room, phone in hand. For the past two days she has stopped herself from making this call. In fact, she promised Joel she wouldn't, ostensibly conceding that she works too hard already. That her achievements are unparalleled therefore unsurpassable; that Ariana, newly eighteen and not going to college, needs Ruth now more than ever. Breaking the promise is not ideal. Wasting Joel's trust, his boyish openheartedness, is like letting organic produce spoil in the fridge. But the betrayal also feels correct, or at least inevitable. Each milestone of Ruth's career to date was enabled by a moment of selfishness. Someone was always watching her from a doorframe, sad eyes saying *I wish you wouldn't.*

Joel is waiting for her in the lobby, intent on making their nine o'clock dinner reservation. He texts her, *almost ready?* She assures him she'll be right down. Finally, Ruth taps her boss's name and lifts the phone to her ear. Phillip is still at the arena prepping the production truck for tomorrow, but he will answer her call. He always does.

When Ruth was thirty-six—the same year she trusted her mother to take Ariana shopping for her first bra, rooting for something sporty, something made of spandex; they came back with an Almost A-Cup Princess Push-up—she was the first woman to announce a nationally-televised NBA game. Lakers versus the Knicks, Madison Square Garden. Until then, Ruth had covered NBA games as a sideline reporter, her experience as an announcer limited to college and WNBA games. It was her privilege that night to escape the camera and retreat to the booth. Freed from her usual tasks of chasing injured players to the locker room, of eavesdropping on huddles and interviewing agitated coaches, she lost herself in the game. When it was over she was a hot air balloon of elation. "Killed it," was the consensus of everyone at the network. ("Is that a girl talking?" was the confused refrain in living rooms across America.) Delusional with triumph, Ruth waited for her boss to draw up a fresh contract. A full season in the analyst's chair, maybe? She'd have signed in a heartbeat.

The network's conclusion was that Ruth now could (and should and should want to) do everything. They still assigned her to the booth during college tournaments, then back to the sideline for the NBA finals. She was the network's go-to analyst for All-Star Weekend and Team USA and Summer League—their reporter for March Madness and Midnight Madness. Now it is Ruth who presents the trophy to the champions in June. Ruth who appears on news programs and podcasts and behind-the-scenes specials.

A year ago, when she was inducted into the Basketball Hall of Fame, the fulcrum of Ruth's acceptance speech was Ariana. Why? Ari, as a rule, does not care about basketball. It's not as if she gave her mother permission to travel the country, to miss Christmases and school concerts, first periods and first heartbreaks. Certainly, at the apex of childhood, when Ariana most loved her mother and least respected Ruth's autonomy—when she still thought nothing of blowing her nose into Ruth's sweater—she would have withheld permission, given the chance. And yet, at that podium in Springfield, Ruth was overwhelmed with gratitude for her teenage daughter. Raised by Ruth's mother and Lester's mother and classmates' mothers. By teachers and babysitters and occasionally Ruth herself. Ariana had survived.

Her work is more than the sum of its parts. It's a thrill Ruth never imagined when she was a shaggy-haired, acne-prone point guard. Even now that the creases between her eyebrows have deepened—her voice crackling at a doleful octave that causes her to clear her throat every time she hears it played back—the assignments have not stopped or slowed.

Today is the last day of May. Ruth's contract is up in October. She has never gotten anything in this business without asking for it.

Phillip answers on the second ring. Over the years his voice has changed, too, the nodes cystic from so much shouting. Now he sounds like he is eternally recovering from bronchitis.

"What's up, RD?"

"This is a serious call," she warns him.

"I consider myself a serious man."

In public, her producer calls her *RD*. If he's had more than a few energy drinks, he calls her *girl*. As in, "Hey, girl" or "Girl, I got you." They are both in their forties, him late, her early. She doesn't mind the shtick—at times, the shtick fuels her—but she appreciates the respect that seeps into his voice as he addresses her by name.

"Ruth. What can I do for you?"

She closes her eyes and swallows against the pressure in her throat, trying to harness the high she felt this afternoon when

Emory Turner agreed to slip behind one of the black curtains honeycombing the Media Day ballroom and to speak to her, her alone, about playing against his best friend and former teammate in the NBA finals. In her mind she replays Turner's comment: "Darius is my brother, but for the next four games he's my enemy."

His tone was serious, sincere, and yet it was hard to believe him. She still pictured Emory Turner and Darius Lake in matching forest-green warm-ups, hands over their hearts for "The Star-Spangled Banner," or sweat-slicked post-game and sabotaging each other's interviews with unsolicited details. Two perpetual groomsmen.

"Four?" Ruth asked. "You're predicting a sweep?"

Known for his mix of vulnerability and cockiness, Emory was in fine form today. Sitting with his knees splayed: "Two here, two in Cincinnati, and I'll see you next season."

Sequestered with the Supersonics star forward, a once-in-a-generation talent, she felt herself professionally invincible. Now she feels as though she's exposing to her boss some unsavory side of Ruth Devon—a drug habit, a kink—but she presses on, delivering the lines she rehearsed in the shower.

"Lester's leaving. I want his job. Of course, you're going to hear from a lot of guys who want his job, but I believe"—she takes a stabilizing breath— "that I've earned it. You know I love the sideline, but I'm ready to call those games."

Her gravitas does not faze Phillip, a man known for karaoke, for restless leg syndrome, for his full head of salt-and-pepper hair. The average NBA fan may not know his name, but he is the ghostwriter of the league, telling a story you thought told itself.

"You're right. All the guys want Les's spot. You're not the first person to call me up. But I hear you, Ruth. You know I hear you. An offer's going out next month—and that's all I can say right now. Can you hang tight until then?"

All the tension leaves her shoulders. Asking is the hardest part.

On paper, Ruth is not qualified for a full-time analyst role. She has never coached or played for an NBA team. Truth be told, she was never qualified for any of this—a realistic goal would have been a few years of regional sideline reporting, fluff pieces and humanizing tidbits, until the season her makeup artist admitted defeat.

"I can hang," she says.

Were it possible for a woman to meet the job's requirements, Ruth would. Either the network is willing to break the mold for her or they're not. Ruth takes nothing for granted and resents no one. Maintaining her pride is a priority.

Phillip laughs.

"What's funny?" she asks.

"Ruth Devon vying for her ex-husband's job. You think he sees what's coming?"

"I'm not a betting woman," Ruth says, "but I'll tell you this: Lester never does."

Joel claims to love Ruth best on vacation mornings. Limp hair knotted, no makeup, underwear lines discernible through the threadbare butt of her sweatpants as she rises from the couch for more coffee. And yet when she catches him looking at her like she's a prize he has won, they are always in a hip restaurant in a newly gentrified neighborhood—her lipstick fresh, complexion smooth in the candlelight. Tonight, after their server uncorks a two-hundred-dollar bottle of

Sancerre, Joel raises his glass and says to Ruth, "You know, some-times I find it hard to believe you have an eighteen-year-old kid."

Joel Fernandez is six years younger than Ruth and has never been married. The year Ariana was born, he was still hemming his Dickies with safety pins, abusing his eardrums in unlicensed clubs, and letting friends pierce his body parts backstage. Frequently his band's set was cut short by the Redondo Beach police department. As the officers elbowed their way through the mosh-pit, The Unholy Messes upped their tempo, racing through the final chorus.

Ruth makes Joel divulge more details of his youth than he would otherwise volunteer. Their childhoods were so different—his lawless, hers ruled by the seasons of organized sports. Did teen-age Joel ever dream that the low-budget record label he and his bandmates founded after high school would ultimately sign some of the biggest artists of the new millennium? That on his thirtieth birthday, he would sell his stake in the company and open a chain of luxury hotels dotting the West Coast?

No more than Ruth could have dreamed up her own life.

She knows he means well, but the compliment—that she does not *look* like a mom—is one she hears often, and never guiltlessly.

"Believe it," Ruth says. "I have the migraines and the Google search history to prove it."

"What have you been searching?"

"Average salary of a woman without a college degree. What models do when they're no longer young. What models do if they get pregnant. Sexual assault in modeling industry. Drug use in model-ing industry. Signs my teenager is on drugs. Signs my teenager—"

"Is fine."

"Signs I've failed as a mother."

"Signs you need a vacation?"

"Signs I will never sleep again."

As their server delivers a shareable heap of squid ink cavatelli to the table, Joel says, "Ariana is going to do great. That picture she sent you? That was so sweet. I would never have sent my mom a picture like that."

He means the group shot of Ariana and her friends getting ready for prom. With a Sephora's worth of powder redefining their features, the girls looked like proud, prize-winning cats. Ruth often fantasizes about scrubbing her daughter's face clean—but who is she to talk? Without the transformative hour in the makeup chair, she would reflexively duck from the camera's view.

Two years ago Ruth was nervous about introducing this man in his thirties to her daughter, whose facial symmetry had already attracted thousands of followers on Instagram. Though Ruth has no way of knowing if Joel complied, she was adamant that he meet Ariana in person before looking her up. Her hope was that he would register Ari as a lanky child, with her father's goofy sense of humor and her mother's pimples, before consuming the airbrushed, angled idea of her. Joel, to his credit and Ruth's comfort, does seem to view Ariana as the kid she is. When he visits them in DC he pretends to confuse Snapchat and TikTok, Kanye and Jay-Z, playing the fool for Ariana and her friends. "Turn down that techno!" he cried when Ari blasted the Chainsmokers through the car speakers, and "What's that—overalls?" when she came downstairs in a Marc Jacobs romper.

"Is she upset about you maybe missing her graduation?" Joel asks.

"I think she's immune to my absence, to be honest. We're always apart for two or three weeks during the playoffs. But *I'm* upset. Somehow, until I saw the schedule, it didn't occur to me that I might not be there for the ceremony."

"Couldn't you back out of Game Seven, if it happens?" Joel asks. "Give some other reporter a chance to shine?"

"No."

"Why not?" He bows his head plate-ward. Joel's tone is overly casual. Was he, in fact, suspicious of the phone call? She knows he wasn't lingering outside the hotel room door—she listened for the ding and descent of the elevator. But maybe he never believed her promise in the first place. Maybe, deep down, he expects her to go after Les's job. It's almost appealing, that he might know her better than her promises.

"Career suicide," she says.

That she's not pursuing a spot in the booth is a lie that will, most likely, be absorbed by the outcome. Ruth has no reason to think she will get those games. As her voice approaches Hubie Brown levels of husk—the problem being that she is not Hubie Brown—her new contract is liable to include less airtime, not more.

"On the subject of"—Joel rotates his fork in the air—"momentous occasions . . ."

When men use the kiss cam to propose to their girlfriends, the girlfriends give one of two effective answers: "Yes for real" or "Yes until halftime." Ruth is haunted by the visible trauma of the second group. What motivates men to turn a simple question into a high-stakes spectacle? Ruth supposes it's the roar of the arena, the uncontained enthusiasm they figure might as well be for them.

"This isn't a proposal, I promise. Although, God, my heart is pounding." He takes a yogi's breath in through his nose, out through his mouth. "I think we should consider getting married. I mean, I want you to consider getting married. To me. I love you exponentially. I'm sold."

Her right hand locates his left. With a gentle application of pressure, she urges him to calm down. Joel's nonproposal is a nonsurprise; the question has been in the purse of his lips, the tilt of his head, for months.

"I love you too. But marriage—or at least, being married to me—might not be what you think it is."

Blushing, and with a mouthful of wine, Joel squeezes and releases her hand. "No spoilers, please. I've never done it before."

"There's a lot of paperwork."

"That's life, baby."

"I'll look old in a wedding dress."

"Yet young in your bridal sweats."

"Aren't we skipping a few steps? You could move to DC. We could start by living together."

"You're not in DC more often than anywhere else."

"I'm there all July."

"Not if you work the summer league."

"Children," she says, planting her glass on the table with exaggerated force. She is laughing but she means it. "You're young. You could still have some with someone else."

"Maybe I could have some with you! You don't know."

At forty-two, Ruth has a slim chance of conceiving naturally. Beyond that, the risk of miscarriage, stillbirth, or fetal abnormality would be too high for comfort. Her period is an erratic guest; she can't remember the last time she reached down and felt the slickness of ovulation. It would seem her body made the decision on her behalf. It's over. She is, as certain moms on the playground used to say with a self-deprecating/self-righteous laugh, "one and done."

Still, she asks Joel, "Do you *want* to have some with me?"

Historically, Joel's attitude toward fatherhood has been noncommittal. Last year, pinned to the couch with his former bandmate's newborn on his chest, Joel's bliss was feminine and palpable—he looked at Ruth with an unhinged grin, already googling *IVF therapy* in his mind. She has witnessed him with his sister's kids—the automatic sinking to his knees upon greeting them, his precise awareness of each toddler's motor skills and whether the adult nearest the staircase ought to intervene. But when Ruth points out that by dating her Joel is delaying, if not missing, his opportunity to reproduce, he smiles and pulls her close. "Isn't that for the best? The world is on fire." Or: "Every day, my sister steps on a Lego. What kind of life is that?"

Now he says, "I always thought your mind was made up on that front. But we could talk about kids. If that's a conversation you want to have, we can have it."

When Ruth married Lester she had every intention of bearing at least three children. Her body, built for jump shots and speed, embraced the challenges of pregnancy. Birth was brutal but she had healed fast. Even when she began traveling for assignments, relying on her mother to babysit and on Lester to swallow his proliferation of objections, she still meant to sneak another baby into her twenties. A second pregnancy was, in Ruth's mind, non-negotiable—until the moment Lester requested a divorce. And even then, she remained open to the possibility of another. By the time she turned thirty-five she had a secret habit of perusing a sperm bank's digital catalog—which allowed customers to organize the donors by height, race, eye color, favorite hobby, and level of education—before logging out, thumbs atremble. By forty, when well-intentioned female colleagues said Ruth was smart to have only one child—and so young!—Ruth experimented with agreement. After all, Ariana had survived her mother's ambition. Why roll the maternity dice again?

Joel says, "How about this? We elope. You sell your house and move to California. Ariana will probably want to be out west eventually, anyway." Ruth dislikes the flippancy with which Joel speaks of Ariana's budding modeling career. "We can do this"—Joel points from his plate to hers—"whenever we please, but at home. Our home. Say you don't want it."

A baby would thwart their dinner plans, Ruth thinks. But Joel has moved on from the subject of babies.

"I want it," Ruth tells him. She has never struggled to want. She has never looked at him and not admired his high cheekbones, full lips, and asymmetrical brow. She has never entered a room and been disappointed to find him in it. When he laughs at one of Ariana's ironically wholesome jokes—*dad jokes*, her friends call them—Ruth's pleasure is unequivocal.

His eyebrows disappear behind his curls. "You do?"

"To be honest, I'm not sure about getting married again. I told myself I wouldn't. But for you, I'm willing to reconsider."

Joel spears two pieces of inky cavatelli. Before delivering the bite to his mouth, he says, "I think the next few years could be great. Maybe even . . . the best?"

Ruth meets his gaze and tells him the truth, which is that she agrees.

GAME ONE

Seattle, Washington

WILDCATS – SUPERSONICS

0–0

CHAPTER THREE

In the morning Ruth repents for last night's wine. The first glass she sipped but the second coincided with Joel suggesting marriage; she gulped it. Now, the sandpaper tongue. The stuffed left nostril and localized headache suggesting she slept with one temple pressed against stone. Lately, Ruth's body begrudges her every whim—beverages, but also desserts and overzealous workouts and popcorn microwaved at midnight. Ruth would like to tell her body, *we are not that old*. Look at the man we are with; look at the hours we keep! Remember the gynecologist noting, "Ruth appears younger than her stated age."

The number alone denotes nothing. Forty-two is an Instagram influencer with toned abs and cleavage up to her neck. Forty-two is someone's grandma. For men, forty-two is the rom-com's male lead, the bank commercial's hot dad—whereas a woman can be a *young* forty-two or an *old* forty-two or, at forty-two, invisible. Often Ruth finds herself comparing her body to her mother's at the same age. Cheryl Landon's abdomen was pale dough cinched by caesarian scar tissue. Long hairs sprouted from her neck and grew like weeds until her fingers found them, gripped, and ripped. Dark, unruly tufts escaped the hollows of her armpits, the elastic of her underwear. As a child Ruth was neither awed nor repulsed by her mother's body. Her mother's body was something she involuntarily memorized, like a map on the wall.

Ruth's own body is something to be conquered.

Joel has a lunch meeting in San Diego, the next city tapped for a Hotel Juniper. As Joel showers and shaves, Ruth stays in bed, curled around her laptop and searching Second Spectrum for film of Darius Lake's playoff assists. When Joel kisses her goodbye, he tastes as he smells—like spearmint and eucalyptus and pipe tobacco. The products Joel buys from his hipster barber, the man responsible for Joel's curls hovering perpetually at his eyebrows, never sheep-dogging into his eyes, always make Ruth nostalgic for a decade they did not live through. Which, she supposes, is the point.

"I wish I had time for breakfast," Joel says.

"Don't worry about it. I have to be at the arena in an hour."

"Meetings?"

"Meetings. Interviews. Shootaround."

"Good luck tonight. Maybe I'll turn on the TV when I get home."

He is not kidding. On the question of whether he will tune into Game One of the NBA finals, from the sideline of which his celebrity girlfriend will be reporting, Joel Fernandez, straight man in America, is a maybe.

He leaves and the door locks itself. At the top of Ruth's Twitter feed is a tweet Emory Turner sent shortly after midnight:

> Let's get it! Game 1. 1 win. Gotta see @HeyRD for that walkout.

Gritted teeth emoji. Prayer hands emoji. Retweets already in the thousands.

Ruth is often asked what it's like to be a lady with a ponytail sidling up to seven-foot All-Stars, daring to pry into their emotions, their insecurities, their hopes. Her work offends a certain kind of man who considers the world of professional sports his last refuge from womankind. If Ruth is feeling generous, she can almost sympathize. Everyone wants to be an expert on something. Used to be that every man felt safe assuming his sports knowledge surpassed every woman's. For most of Ruth's career, the industry merely tolerated her. Aging analysts in their flamboyant suits would slap their hands against the studio desk: "Can we talk about Ruth Devon? I'm no sexist, I just don't want to listen to her call a game she can't play. Keep that girl on the sideline, is all I'm saying." Ruth spent summers sucking in her breath, panic-planning an alternate life, convinced her access to her own life would be abruptly denied. But the network could not let her go—she was too prepared, too reliable. Quick on her feet and good in a crisis. An NBA encyclopedia in heels, Ruth became a fan favorite gradually. A household name suddenly.

Her official explanation, trotted out in interviews, is that she crossed her arms and refused to leave; over time, the world relented. A more popular theory involves a Canadian rapper's bespoke T-shirt, emblazoned with her Warholed face. He wore it to a game and asked her out to dinner on national television. He advised her to "come alone."

What Ruth believes is that the players noticed her first. They noticed her tailor-made questions informed by their stats, histories, and past comments. They appreciated the maternal placement of her hand on their backs. Her disarming, deliberate eye contact. It was Emory Turner who first matched her gaze and, with the red light as his witness, thanked her by name. Several years ago, while filming an endorsement for the network, Emory was asked to list his top five basketball personalities. He mentioned Ruth first. "She always asks you a question you're down to answer. We all have our preferences when it comes to the media, but no one's ever upset to see Ruth. She's our girl. She's the goat."

A colleague had sent her the clip before it aired. She watched it, smiling up until the last line. In a text to Ariana:

> Good or bad if Emory Turner calls me a goat?

Ariana wrote back:

> Greatest! Of! All! Time! 🐐 🕴 🐷🐐

Six months ago, Ruth sat down with Emory in the locker room following his first game without Darius Lake. "It's always hard to lose a teammate," Ruth said. "But you and Darius played eight seasons together. Four playoff runs, two trips to the finals against Orlando. I remember talking to him after a game last season, and you interrupted Darius to ask if you could borrow his deodorant."

"Not the deodorant he was using. Dude keeps about three things of Old Spice in his bag. Unopened. Says he doesn't like to sweat."

Ruth laughed. "That's—"

"Peculiar, I know."

"It was only a few years ago that the Sonics urged Lake to re-sign with the whole . . ."

Emory sighed. "The ceremony."

The team owners had summoned Lake to the arena, leading him through a makeshift walkway, the walls of which were collaged in his image. They hoisted his jersey to the rafters while a gospel choir sang a saccharine version of "Run This Town." Did the whole spectacle sound absurd, superfluous? Yes.

Does Ruth wish she had been there? Also yes.

"When Darius re-signed with Seattle, we all understood his loyalty was to the city, to the franchise, and to you. Can you tell me about the moment you learned you were no longer teammates?"

Emory was sitting with a towel draped over his head. He pushed it back to look Ruth in the eye. "My phone rang. Three a.m. Sasha's sleeping in bed next to me, so I go to the bathroom and I sit down. And Darius says, 'Man, I got traded. They traded me for Kasey.'" Emory dug two fingers into the grooves of his forehead. His account of the phone call exposed the serrated edges of his grief, his barely-contained anger at Seattle's front office. He didn't yet know the Supersonics would face the Wildcats in the finals and couldn't have processed the outcome even if he had, somehow, been warned. It was bad enough to know that the general managers, in spite of their elaborate gestures, would play their lives like the stock market.

"I had to drop my head between my knees to stop the room from spinning. It was worse than a concussion. Worse than . . ."

Ruth thought back to Turner's rookie season, cut short by a torn patellar tendon. Nineteen years old, he had crumpled to the floor, a horse-wild look in his eyes. Over and over in a haunted monotone: "I'm fucking done. I'm fucking done." The telecast's audio had lapsed.

"Well, you know," he finished.

If Joel hadn't already left for San Diego, this is when Ruth would ask him to confiscate her screens before she could pore over the replies to Emory's tweet. Social media is a necessary tool for tracking industry drama, but she tries to avoid her own mentions. Posts need to be both viral and flattering before she will respond. When a high school girl tweeted a picture of herself dressed as Ruth Devon for Halloween, Ruth offered to loan her an outfit next year. When a college player's friends filmed him high on laughing gas after dental surgery, raving about her beauty and prowess, Ruth wrote, "Wishing this young man a speedy recovery!" She thought the "young man" was a nice touch, erring on the side of matronly for her daughter's benefit.

To Emory Turner, she tweets, "See you tonight!" with a heart and a hashtag: #letstipitup. She suspects Emory has motives beyond flattering her. She doesn't mind. If she can relieve some of the pressure heading into Game One, Ruth is happy to assist.

The pressure must be immense. Because the trade that broke up the NBA's most prominent bromance did not break Darius Lake. Instead, it resulted in a puzzling, stunning breakthrough. Halfway through Game Seven of the Eastern Conference Finals, Lester called Ruth at home. He called on the landline she had been meaning to disconnect, it rang so rarely. He greeted her with, "Correct me if I'm wrong—"

"I will," she promised.

"During last year's finals, Lake was shooting thirty-five percent from the field."

"That sounds right."

"Turner appeared to be on the verge of drawing up divorce papers."

"It was an emotional series for the Sonics."

"But tonight, one year and one mind-fuck of a trade later, Darius 'King of the Midrange' Lake has made six three-pointers."

Ruth carried the phone back to the living room and sank into the couch. She muted the rival network's telecast, preferring Lester's uncensored commentary in her ear. For them it was a night off; they had already wrapped up their coverage of the games out west. Joel had gone upstairs to watch *The Bachelor* with Ariana. In his absence, Ruth could relax into the rhythm of the game, no longer obligated to find her boyfriend's questions clever ("Do the refs ever get power-hungry?" "Do the players smell bad after?") and her reactions to each play freed from Joel's ironic scrutiny. She loved the man, but he needed to stay the hell off her couch during the playoffs.

"Correct me if I'm wrong," Lester repeated, "but the Wildcats are about to win this."

"Shut your mouth," Ruth said. "Five minutes to go."

On cue, Orlando combusted. This was their conference and their game to win. They were set on a three-peat with the Sonics as their worthy competitors—not these wide-eyed Wildcats reliant on Seattle's castoffs. 5.2 seconds on the clock, the score tied, and Lester stopped speaking. The phone was hot against Ruth's ear. Darius dribbled along the perimeter, stopped in front of his own bench, and let it fly from thirty feet. The ball bounced twice on the near side of the rim.

Twice more on the far side of the rim.

The ball fell through the net.

Darius Lake has been called *the Stoic*. He has been described as detached, emotionless—a robot programmed to pose as a human athlete. A space alien blundering his way through earthly transactions. Rumors abound: that he skips postgame celebrations in favor of *Friends* reruns at home; that he still drives his Chevy Elantra from high school. In Ruth's opinion, the characterization is overblown, designed to provoke a young man who remains shy in an industry fueled by fame. Still, it was breathtaking, his understated reaction to sinking the buzzer-beating three that won the Eastern Conference Finals. Darius Lake did not scream. He did not cry. He did not fall to the floor, euphoric and spent.

He nodded.

The fourth wall of the telecast crumbled: cameramen swarmed the court; reporters seized their mics; coaches delivered congenial blows to each other's backs. Ruth was a thousand miles from the Amway Center but she could feel the vibrations of the court in her calves. Her eardrums flinched, bracing for an onslaught that wasn't coming. Her eyes followed Darius as his teammates mauled him. At last Sondra Lake shoved her way onto the floor, and Darius enveloped his mother in arms that could have wrapped around her twice. Sondra, a retired schoolteacher from Compton, once lingered in a media scrum to pull Ruth aside and wish her a happy Mother's Day, a kindness so unexpected Ruth had teared up on the spot.

Ruth was watching in her softest sweats and oldest Georgetown T-shirt. She should have been happy for this brief reprieve before the finals—a few days among her people, a few nights in her own bed. In the morning she was going to fire up the lawnmower and conquer the grass caressing the sides of the house. Ariana had threatened to hire landscapers, but Ruth reserved the task for herself, relishing the sun on her shoulders, the heft of the machine, the visible progress. Sometimes she fantasized about mowing the local baseball field, doing the lines and the bases, so that it would be pristine for upcoming Little League games. Thinking of the lawnmower dormant in the garage, Ruth was happy—and she had nearly forgotten she was still on the phone when she heard Lester clear the emotion from his throat.

"What would you give to get that interview with Lake?"

She laughed and told him what he already knew.

CHAPTER FOUR

Two hours before tip-off, deep in the arena's underground, Ruth slips inside a dressing room. Angie, the network's senior stylist, has already unpacked and arranged her supplies: the foundations and blushes and shadows, the cupfuls of brushes, the ceramic irons and combs.

"Are we alone?" Ruth asks, her voice amplified by the high ceilings.

"Completely. We're basically quarantined. Even I had trouble finding this place."

For what feels like the first time today, Ruth sits. Angie pulls the elastic from Ruth's ponytail and examines the blond ends of her hair. "Good," she says. "You've been using the conditioner."

"It makes me smell like yogurt."

"Nope." Angie shakes her head. "It makes you smell like coconut and cardamom seeds."

Angie's look changes every few weeks. Though the transformations are dramatic, they are also so frequent Ruth no longer notices whether Angie's hair is turquoise or maroon, partially shaved or woven into extensions. For herself, Ruth wants the opposite effect: an appearance so unchanging, viewers are tricked into admiring that which is clearly, dependably, under control.

For years Ruth was tasked with her own beautification: alone in a hotel room, contorting her arms behind her head to iron her hair. She's glad to have bequeathed the responsibility to someone else. And Ruth trusts Angie, the way you trust the woman in whose hands your porous, cavernous face—ravaged by airplane air and sleep deprivation—becomes camera-ready. The trust is essential: Ruth will use her hour in the chair to call her daughter.

Players have their pregame rituals. There's the jittery point guard who insists on making a shot from the tunnel, a full fifty feet away; the sixteen-time All-Star who heaps powdered chalk in each palm before tossing the dust in the air, arms flung crucifixion-wide; the player who pounds his head against the stanchion of the basket, obliterating non-game-related thoughts; the veteran who massages the ball as if loosening the peel from an orange. Likewise, Ruth needs to hear Ariana's voice in the hours before tip-off; she needs it with her whole twitching, flinching body. Because once the clock is running, Ruth knows she won't think of her daughter at all.

In the regular season, when she returns home for three- or four-day stretches between games, she sustains her momness. She wears jeans and hosts sleepovers and schedules dentist appointments to preserve Ariana's second and final set of teeth. She eats dinner with her daughter. She asks her daughter to please not leave wet towels on the carpet in her room. She has time to worry she's raised a shallow girl, a vain girl, a flimsy girl—only to end the night laughing helplessly into Ariana's hard shoulder, assured of the kid's sweetness and hilarity, the warmth she inherited from her dad. But in the postseason, when Ruth is on the road for weeks at a time, she forgets her maternity the way New Yorkers visit Los Angeles and never take their balled-up sweaters from their suitcases. It's involuntary and inevitable: she forgets what her daughter is like.

Lately, Ariana has tended toward suburban transience, drifting from one Maryland McMansion to another. Sleeping in a series of luxurious, generic guest rooms and washing her hair with shampoo selected by someone else's mom. Consequently, Ruth never knows where her daughter will be when she picks up the phone. Tonight, Ruth is pleased to learn that Ariana is at home with her grandmother.

"How was prom, sweetie? Was the after-party fun? Was Chandler there?"

"Prom was fine. The party sucked and, yeah, Chandler was there. The two things are probably related."

"Chandler is the reason the party sucked?"

"The parties never change, and Chandler never changes, either. I'm thinking maybe I'm done with things that don't change."

Ruth refrains from pumping a fist in the air. She has nothing personal against Chandler, whom she is fairly certain she could identify from a lineup of young men named after nineties sitcom characters. She is always relieved when her daughter breaks it off with another boy.

"You should have come to Seattle with me." Days ago, Ruth tried and failed to coax Ariana out west for Game One. Ariana declined the invitation repeatedly, her stubbornness opaque. The last game she had attended was a season-opener in Orlando. Ruth was actually calling that one, in the booth alongside play-by-play announcer Marcus Keen. At the start of the third, Marcus said, "We have a handful of celebrities in the house tonight, but none so important as this young lady." The broadcast cut to a shot of

Ariana seated a few rows up from the floor, hunched over her phone, obliviously scratching at a zit on her nose. "There's Ariana, Ruth's daughter," Marcus said. The tribute delighted Ruth. She had seen her daughter on the booth's monitor and thought she looked beautiful, if bored.

Ariana, after a friend tweeted the clip, seethed for days.

"See, the thing is," she says now, "I don't actually *like* basketball."

"But you like me. And I'm here." Ruth knows she is fishing for affection from her teenage daughter; the desired result is so satisfying, Ruth feels no shame.

"I do like you," Ariana agrees. "And it would have been nice to get out of here. Speaking of which: there's something you should know."

Ruth steels herself. "All right."

"I'm going to LA in July."

"No," Ruth says reflexively but without conviction. If she fights Ariana, she will lose every time. It's tepid support that sometimes works out in her favor.

"Yes. Manny booked me a shoot for Brandy Melville."

"Can I come?" The first week of July is Ruth's break before the start of summer league. The fantasy of spending her vacation in LA with her daughter unspools rapidly in the seconds between the request and Ariana's answer.

"No, Mom, this is a real job. An editorial shoot with a real contract. I can't bring my mother with me. It would be like you bringing Grandma to a game. You'd be like, 'He shoots! He scores! Nothing but net, hoo-wee!' And Grandma would be like, 'Honey, it's a little bit cold in here—did you bring a sweater?'"

It's deliberately inaccurate, Ari's impression of her job. Still Ruth laughs, provoking Angie into threatening her with an eyeliner pencil.

Accepting or at least resigning herself to Ariana's modeling career is an act of will that takes daily recommitment. It started when Ariana was fourteen. It started, in Ruth's opinion, innocently enough, with makeup tutorials uploaded to YouTube. There was an intriguing honesty to those early videos, the way they began with Ariana's face naked and blemished. Narrating every brush-stroke in her world-weary tenor, Ari painted on her shimmering contoured disguise. Back then, the fights about her future were messy and unsophisticated. Ari bellowed the usual refrains—Ruth was a tyrant, a prison warden—and Ruth countered with stock phrases of parental authority, none of which satisfied her daughter, much less Ruth herself. As Ariana grew into a young woman, shrewd and perceptive, she learned to exploit her mother's weakness: basketball.

Ruth had maintained that Ariana was going to college, and for a long time Ariana had no retort; it was an expectation held by all her friends' parents. Until the day it dawned on Ari that only a fraction of the players in the league Ruth so revered had finished school before declaring their eligibility for the draft. Turned out, invoking the NBA invalidated most of Ruth's arguments against modeling: that Ari shouldn't tie her living to her body; that her health would be destroyed by the strain of long hours and travel; that she needed a viable and meaningful career after the age of thirty.

Ruth remembers pressing the small of her back against the kitchen counter, removing her glasses to massage the bridge of her nose, a cliché of maternal exasperation. Professional sports are, yes, a commodification of the body. Like supermodels, NBA stars take out insurance plans on their limbs. Both athleticism and beauty are gifts of genetics, randomly bestowed—but capitalizing on those gifts takes commitment, discipline, work. Ruth had played the game until her body failed her; given half a chance, she would do it again, even if she knew the result would not change. (Always, in the end, howling on the floor, cradling her blown-out knee.) Ruth knows this much about herself, and Ariana knows this much about her mother.

Ruth would have liked to say: "So what?" What's good enough for Ruth is not, by extension, good enough for Ariana. To depend on your body's excellence is to risk the *pop* of ruination, which you will register even before the pain sets in, and which will render the pain secondary to the grief. Ruth would do anything to spare her daughter that *pop*—or the analogous moment in a model's career, which Ruth, for all her fretting, cannot begin to imagine.

On her eighteenth birthday Ariana signed with a DC-based agency and was assigned to Manny, a booker whose verbal tic is to say "beautiful" in place of "okay" or "sure." Ruth had never seen her daughter prouder than when pulling up the agency's home page and presenting the screen for Ruth's approval. It took Ruth a harrowing few seconds to locate Ari's headshot among the rows of air-brushed faces. Finally, her eyes alighted on Ariana's hair. (Those curls, Ruth has never gotten over them.) Alarm bells clanged in her head. Too late.

As Angie slides Ruth's glasses over the bridge of her nose, Ruth prepares to end the call. "I'm not going to crash your trip. I was just teasing."

Truthfully, Ruth is desperate to watch Ariana work—both to ensure no one lays a finger on her, and because her curiosity knows no bounds. How does her daughter the model behave? How do photographers and assistants and advertisers behave toward her daughter the model? Still, every time Ariana denies her the opportunity to find out, Ruth is relieved. Since she was very small, Ari has lived a life of which Ruth has only a partial view. She has learned about her daughter from report cards and babysitters, by stealing glances at the texts proliferating on Ari's screen. Now that her child is a legal adult, Ruth isn't sure how much she wants to know.

She isn't sure how much she deserves to know.

"So I was wondering . . ." Gloom has lowered Ariana's voice. Ruth braces herself. She needs to turn her mind toward the game, to metaphorically bang her head against the stanchion. "Yes?"

"Are you, like, for sure not coming to my graduation?"

Ruth's heart seems to clench.

When Ariana was eight, she went through a phase of expressing absolute bereavement every time her mother left town for a game. In her bare feet and nightgown, she would chase Ruth to the driveway and try to wrestle her suitcase from the cabdriver before he could load it into the trunk. Her sobs were frayed, feral, and they merged with high-pitched screams that sawed at the cords of Ruth's motivation. If not for her own mother's tender firmness as she appeared in the driveway—fully dressed, no matter the hour—and carried Ariana back inside, Ruth would have caved. She'd have canceled her contract and stayed home every time.

Instead, she climbed into the taxi feeling light-headed and dissociative. She would watch the clock on the dashboard and try to guess the minute at which Ariana had heaved her last sob. Surely, by the time the cab turned onto the parkway, Cheryl had distracted Ari with cartoons or frozen waffles. And surely, by the time Ruth pushed through the terminal's revolving door, Ariana's face bore the ghost of her anguish—dusty streaks beneath her eyes, a fading rash on her neck.

"It's still too early to say, baby."

"Okay. Except I realized I really want you there. Dad's coming, and it's going to be so depressing having dinner alone with him after."

"Lester said he's coming?"

"Yeah. No matter what."

But Lester is contractually obligated to call a Game Seven if there is one—*no matter what*. That he's gambled on the lie does not surprise Ruth, but now she needs to smack him.

"Since when is spending time with your father depressing?"

"Since his girlfriend dumped him and he says things like, 'Better to be over the hill than under it, right, kiddo?' while staring at the wall like a neutered dog."

"Gwen dumped Lester?" Ruth glances at Angie, who has a hairpin between her teeth and does not react.

"Uh-huh. She told Dad she wants a second act."

"What does that mean, exactly?"

"New man. Babies. The works."

"Gwen wants babies? The woman's in her forties." A retired dancer, Gwen owns a barre studio in Adams Morgan, where she shoves and stretches sinewy women into a series of socket-defying poses. Her lean limbs and augmented lips make her look both younger and older than Ruth.

"I know, it's gross. Dad gets all worked up about it and tells me details I do *not* need to know. That's why I want you there."

"Of course I want to be there, sweetie. But if there's a Game Seven, I have to work it."

"You don't have to," Ariana says. "People get sick. People have family emergencies."

"People do."

"But you don't."

Ruth is silent.

Ariana heaves a sigh. Then, as if her conscience has put a gun to her head: "Have fun tonight, Mom. Maybe next year you'll be calling the game."

Angie is coaxing Ruth's hair into camera-friendly waves when Phillip shoulders through the dressing room door. Close behind him is play-by-play announcer Jay Thomas—known for lingering at the broadcast table after especially breathtaking fourth quarters, his eyes darting between spots on the floor as he mutters a recap of the final play, cramming for some self-administered quiz—followed by color analyst Lester Devon. Together they are the network's highest-rated broadcasting duo. In ongoing celebration of this fact, they like to coordinate their outfits, opting for ties and pocket squares in theatrical patterns that tend to look better with Jay's dark skin than with Lester's pallor. Both men are bald, their heads already oiled or moisturized or powdered, whatever needs to happen there, freeing them up to crash Ruth's hour with Angie.

"How did you find me?" she says.

Phillip is composing a text message. He raises his one-minute finger, a gesture in which his hand will one day freeze.

"We wandered blindly, calling out your name." Lester sinks to a bench behind Ruth's chair but still within her mirrored view.

"We asked Natalie," Jay answers. Their stage manager's knowledge of their whereabouts is so precise, Ruth sometimes wonders if Natalie has tapped their phones.

Phillip fires off a flurry of texts before lowering the screen a healthy six inches from his face. "Okay, RD. What we talked about, where you introduce the Emory-Darius drama and segue into some stats? I'm calling an audible. Turns out Taylor Swift is coming tonight. I want you to talk to her. She's tall, right? Ask if she played in high school—did she go to high school? Ask if she's ever written a song about Emory Turner. No, don't do that. That's sexist, isn't it?"

Ruth makes eye contact with his reflection. Steam rises from the lock of hair clamped in Angie's curling wand. "I'm not sure how tall she is."

"Great. Lead with that."

Ruth wonders if the Swift assignment is, indirectly, the result of last night's call, which they are pretending did not happen. But no—in their afternoon meeting Phillip seemed pleased with Ruth's pitches. If he thinks fans want a screenful of pop star in the minutes before Game One of the NBA finals, he's probably right.

Ruth says, "People are riveted by this Emory-Darius story."

"Lester will compare their stats in the opener. Lake's efficiency, Turner's defense, the ways their games have changed since the trade—don't worry, we're using all that. It's good stuff."

Ruth twists in her chair to look directly at Lester. Angie exhales through her nose. Squeezing his shoulders, Lester exonerates himself: this is out of his control; Phillip is running the show; et cetera.

Ruth's idea was to start with some drama to hook even channel-surfing non-fans: two ex-teammates, formerly the league's most lethal pick-and-roll partnership—whose families vacationed together! Whose daughters attended the same Montessori school in Seattle!—meet again as competitors in the finals. From there, she was going to illustrate the matchup with numbers. And she spent *time* on those numbers, boiling each player's game down to its most effective parts. Too much time, maybe, for a segment that will top out at thirty seconds.

Sensing her resistance, Phillip sighs. He slides his phone into his pocket, stopping short of withdrawing his hand. "Look, Ruth, you're not an analyst tonight. You're a reporter. Taylor Swift posted an Insta story wishing Emory good luck. She pretended she was his coach, like she taught him everything he knows. It was actually quite droll."

Angie gives Ruth's hair a final fluff and begins packing up her tools. Ruth rises from her chair, stomping the lost feeling back into her legs and ignoring her pregame butterflies, more frenzied than usual. "I have nothing against Taylor. I'm sure she's fascinating in her own right. But listen, I sat down with Emory yesterday. The man said, and this is a direct quote, 'Darius is my brother, but for the next four games he's my enemy.'"

Phillip's head droops to one side. "That's good."

"That is good," Lester says. "Turner never gives me anything good. I ask him a question, and he fixes me with this look, this mean fucking look, like he's picturing my head in a toilet."

"Now I'm picturing your head in a toilet," Jay says.

Out of habit, the men are sitting unconventionally close to each other, elbows accustomed to colliding in the booth. "How do I look?" Lester asks.

"Not bad," Jay says.

Ruth pleads her case. "I'll hook them with the drama. I'll quote Turner. And then I'll finish with the stats, like we talked about."

Phillip's salt-and-pepper hair gets saltier as he chews his lip and performs a mental calculation: Taylor Swift's online antics versus Ruth's desperation for airtime.

They are no longer pretending last night's call didn't happen.

"I won't be verbose," Ruth says. "I'll make it punchy and to the point. I'll smile." She gives him a preview of the smile she means—a disarming display of whitened teeth, requiring careful contortion of each part of her face. A process through which Ariana has coached her.

Phillip's pocket vibrates. His one-minute finger seems to rise again, then slices through the air to point at Ruth. "You got it," he says. "Back to the original plan. But in the event that Seattle's up by twenty, let's fit Swift into a segment later on."

"That's fair," Ruth says. But she's not expecting a blowout. Ruth has been obsessed with Darius Lake all season. The trade—which, for a lesser player, might have meant the beginning of the end—unlocked something. The adjustments to his game were barely discernible; it's possible he cleaned up his shot, tightened his right elbow, got more rotation on the ball. But mentally he's transformed. Gone are the moments of hesitation, the long twos, the nail-biting on the bench. As a Wildcat, Darius stays ahead of the play: he gets a touch and makes a judgment in the same instant; blink, and he's either shooting a three or at the rim. The Sonics may have stats and history on their side, but Ruth suspects that Emory, already unpredictable under pressure, will meet his match in his old friend.

Phillip and Angie try to exit the room at the same time. Angie steps back and Phillip passes her with long, self-important strides. Covertly, Ruth appraises her body in the full-length mirror—fine, she looks fine, unless her skirt is too tight across her ass? A week ago it wasn't—before telling Lester and Jay, "I'll see you guys out there."

Hoping no one follows her, she turns down a wide hallway muraled with iconic Emory dunks, passing locker rooms whose precise layouts she could conjure in her sleep. Over the course of her career, Ruth has clocked hundreds of hours in the bowels of this building. Pioneer Center is the oldest structure in the NBA, slated for implosion this summer, the end of an era. Next season, the Supersonics will play in a glossy new arena overlooking the Puget Sound.

Everyone Ruth encounters on her way to the court smiles or gawks at her. In addition to smiling and gawking they say her name—either with proud familiarity or with slack-jawed reverence. "Ruth," says a twenty-six-year-old shooting coach. "Ruuuuth," bleats a bearded beat writer with a popular podcast on which Ruth keeps promising to appear. "Ruth!" chirps Alison Lee, a sideline reporter for Seattle's regional network, known for abusing the talk-back button with unworthy huddle updates. Alison's contract won't be renewed—a bit of gossip Ruth wishes she didn't know. She likes Alison.

Seattle's mascot, a well-groomed, ever-pensive Sasquatch, clasps his hairy hands together and bows mutely at Ruth, implying but not speaking her name.

Then, coming up behind her in the tunnel: the smooth timbre familiar to anyone who has ever patronized a sports bar on a Wednesday night, now drained of the irony with which he protected himself in the dressing room.

"Ruthie. Wait for me."

It's possible to forget that she once kneeled at the altar with Lester Devon, before Catholicism completely lost its grip on her. That she took (and never returned) his name, made his bed, pressed his shirts. She gave birth with the man stationed at her right knee, his attention fixed on the gore between her legs, his spirited narration of the event a precursor to his second career. To forget all that, Ruth must either lock herself in the present moment, taking shelter in their roles for the night (Lester in the analyst's chair, she on the sideline) or go all the way back to college (Lester the coach, she the starting point guard). But the pet name is too much. It pinches a nerve. She hears *Ruthie* and thinks: what's *he* doing here?

They stand alone at the mouth of the tunnel. Already the roar is oceanic.

"You've heard the news?" he asks her.

Most conversations with Lester are about Lester; even so, Ruth hesitates.

"What news?"

He laces his fingers behind his neck. "Come on. I'm abdicating the throne!"

In his late fifties, Lester has reached peak handsomeness. Observing the brightness of his gray eyes, the rough-hewn jaw and easy smile, you might assume his bald dome is a choice. But Ruth knows that by thirty-seven Lester was hiding a geriatric halo of auburn fuzz beneath his baseball cap. By forty a barber was shaving him clean twice a month. If she's honest, Ruth misses the caps. She misses nineties fashion in general—the dressy turtlenecks and billowing khakis. These things looked right to her.

She laughs at him. "Yes. Everyone knows that. You know I know. Why are you asking if I know?"

Lester is unabashed. "You haven't said a word!"

Ruth sometimes worries that her ex-husband's naked need for her attention is what has enabled her to remain unmarried since their divorce. When the boyfriends realize that Ruth Devon is 20 percent maternal anxiety, 80 percent basketball—which is to say, when the boyfriends leave—she only has to call up Lester to hear her name spoken with a combination of thirst and gratitude. That Lester never stopped wanting her was, until she met Joel, the North Star of her personal life. (Some years it was the entirety of her personal life.) Now his affection remains a comfort but also a burden. Several times per season he touches her face, and she pushes him away.

By failing to congratulate him on his retirement, Ruth didn't mean to hurt Lester's feelings. She meant to put some superstitious distance between herself and the subject. She wants Lester's job, but not because it's his. Ruth has wanted a spot in the booth since the days when Lester, a head NBA coach, considered the media a pain in his ass.

Ruth asks, "What was I supposed to say?"

"That you're happy for me? Proud of an old friend? Hoping I'll finally pass on my secrets of the trade?"

"As far as I'm concerned, your leaving is a loss. For the league and for the network. And for me."

Either Lester knows she wants his job and is choosing to say nothing, a display of restraint for which there is no precedent, or he is oblivious—which would be typical.

"I suppose you've heard the other news," Lester says.

"You and Gwen? Ariana just told me. I was sorry to hear it."

"She wants children." Lester turns up his palms. "As if I could jump in a time machine, go back to the eighties, and impregnate her."

"Gwen was a child in the eighties. I'm sure that's not at all what she wants."

Lester blinks. "I'm the one in the time machine, remember? And I was in my twenties. Twenty-six is the perfect age to start a family. When I was twenty-six I could touch my toes. From a standing position, I could literally bend in half and touch my goddamn toes."

"You're nuts," Ruth observes.

"I got a vasectomy after our divorce," Lester says.

They are interrupted by Wildcats center Anthony Moore and his nine-year-old son. "Can Jakob get a pic with you two?" Anthony asks. "He's a big, big fan. Loves you, Ruth."

Ruth's reaction to Lester's comment is still active on her face. She's aware of relaxing her features as she nods at Moore. She doesn't know him well. He's a veteran, just past his prime, who spent nine years in Atlanta before signing with Cincinnati. Born in the Dominican Republic, raised in Michigan, married to a beauty queen. He rarely hits a shot from the perimeter, but when he does he celebrates by miming steeping a tea bag and taking a sip, a gesture that never fails to crack Ruth up.

Lester is already grinning, bending his knees to crouch at kid height, but Jakob presses himself firmly against Ruth. One skinny arm snakes around her midsection, and for a moment Ruth feels she will die if she never has another baby and if the baby is not a boy. A boy, in her imagination, would be like Ruth: restless and competitive and always slightly out of breath. A boy would brag about her career to his friends—something Ariana never considered, preferring the cryptic deflection, "My mom's on TV."

Anthony Moore snaps the photo from his height of seven-two, an aerial shot that must include more of Lester's scalp than his face. Satisfied, Moore passes the phone (pregame contraband) to his son. Jakob is slow to disentangle from Ruth. "You're awesome," he whispers as if it's the salutation of a prayer.

"Sweet kid," Lester says afterward.

"Cutie pie," Ruth agrees. And now she remembers why she feels more annoyed with Lester than usual, why she can't stop hating his tie. "Did you tell Ariana you're going to her graduation?"

"I have every intention of going to her graduation."

"Game Seven?"

"Come on. The Cats won't take the Sonics to seven. This is a safe bet."

"If you're wrong about that, you're on your own, my friend. I'm not doing your dirty work."

Of course she will do his dirty work. How else can she ensure the news is broken to Ariana gently, strategically? Ruth's impassive expression does not waver, even as she endures the physically painful sensation of needing to do two things at once. She needs to tell Ariana she loves her—did she say it during their call, or did she forget?—and she also needs to review her notes before filming her first segment. Lester has robbed her of time to do either. If NBA players are forbidden to check their phones in the minutes before a game, Ruth should be forbidden from talking to her ex-husband.

Lester clamps a coach's hand on her shoulder. "Stop by my room tonight. Don't bring your millennial boyfriend. I want to talk to you."

"Joel is not a millennial," Ruth says. (He is.) "And he's not in town." She should refuse the invitation outright, but instead she squeezes Lester's arm and moves past him. It's nearly game time. What happens in the NBA finals becomes history on a seven-second delay.

For the rest of the night Lester will be the illustrious Lester Devon: beloved former coach, analyst with a bone to pick. The superior whom Ruth may never succeed. For now, she forgets him. She steps onto the floor and waves to Julian, the long-tenured cameraman waiting to film her segment. She catches an errant basketball and chest-passes it to the nearest Sonic still in his forest-green warmups. The player winks. The anticipation of the crowd washes over her, steadies her, propels her heels across the court.

But in the earliest hours of the morning, with her face wiped clean and her hair reponytailed, she will leave her hotel room for Lester's. In the back of her mind, she already knows this.

CHAPTER FIVE

After the Supersonics are introduced—each player's name boomed in the stadium announcer's most menacing, warmongering baritone—artificial fog hangs over the court. Preserved in the vapor is the crowd's anticipation, the remains of their "Star-Spangled Banner" feelings. For Ruth, the fog evokes the NBA games of her father's childhood, when teams would play through a film of cigarette smoke. Ruth likes the effect. Excitement cinches her throat—maybe incongruously, as the first few minutes of the game are ugly. Over the initial turnovers and whistles and missed foul shots, Jay Thomas—audible through a discrete, flesh-toned piece of technology lodged in Ruth's left ear—says, "I guess we should acknowledge the elephant in the room."

Lester: That's a rude way to refer to our friend Anthony Moore.

Jay (chuckling): This is one of your last games as an announcer—oh! Lake gets a good look from the corner and . . . misses it—you're retiring.

Lester: Yeah, yeah, I sure am.

Jay: And what's next for you?

Lester: Oh, I might go back to coaching. Probably not immediately and probably not the NBA. Maybe college.

Jay: Turner drives into the paint, gets to the rim, and that's his
first bucket of the night. You like the kids?

Lester: I love the kids. And speaking of coaching, I'm not the
only golden-ager in the building. I'm assuming you caught the press
release about this being Rick Bellantoni's last season.

Jay: That's right. The Cats won't be the same without him,
will they?

Lester: The league won't be the same without him.

Jay: KP draws the foul and Cincinnati calls their first time-out.
Nor you.

Lester could be bullshitting, Ruth thinks. It wouldn't be the
first time he has explored his career options on-air. (A common
refrain: "This might get me fired, but . . .") He could just as easily
be for real. It's unusual, if not unprecedented, for an NBA coach
to return to college basketball. But what Lester wants, ardently or
on a lark, he will get. The man was the assistant coach of American University's men's team for a mere two years before he was
promoted to head coach. Two years after that, the Washington
Wizards brought him on and Lester ascended the same ranks in,
roughly, the same time frame.

During each of Lester's six seasons with the Wizards, the team
made the playoffs but never advanced past the second round. In
Lester's last game as a coach, Detroit's bruising, seven-foot center
threw a punch at the Wizards' best player, an equally enormous
power forward. It happened in front of the Wizards' bench; Lester
could not let his star retaliate and risk suspension. Diminutive at
five-eleven and some one hundred and sixty pounds, Lester clung
to the calf of the NBA All-Star who dragged him indifferently

across the floor and, in the end, threw a suspension-worthy punch anyway. The Wizards' brain trust, frustrated and frazzled and, perhaps, as Ruth was, haunted by the footage of Lester wrapped around his player's leg like a shy child, turned on him. Lester was fired in June.

So concluded the year during which Ruth, age thirty-six, had called the Knicks-Lakers game at the Garden. She and Lester had long ceased to be spouses or even casual competitors; she took no pleasure—none!—in his disgrace coinciding with her professional breakthrough. Besides, coaches were fired the way players were traded: no hard feelings, management only wanted to mix things up. Lester would find another coaching gig. Ruth had no doubt they would both come out on top.

The following season, when the network whimsically gave Lester a spot in the booth as a guest analyst, then swiftly extended a full-time offer, Ruth was livid, unable to shake the conviction that Lester had stolen something from her. Never had he expressed an interest in broadcasting. Not once had he conceded that Ruth's field required any special skill set or natural talent. Worse, Ruth already knew he would be a fan favorite, with his instantly formed opinions, his encyclopedic knowledge dating back to the seventies. His ties loud yet tasteful, his picket-fence teeth.

Lester did not deserve the job, but the job deserved him. Buzzed on two margaritas from a TGI Fridays in Newark's most desolate terminal—her flight twice delayed—Ruth called him with congratulations.

"Thanks, Ruthie." He sounded cheerful but over-indulged, bloated with other people's praise. "Not my usual beat, but I'm planning to have fun with it. No reason for everything to be so high stakes all the time, right?"

Ruth felt herself go rigid. "Broadcasting comes with its own challenges. The pressure might surprise you."

"You're jealous."

"Sure," Ruth admitted easily. "Full-time color analyst? I've wanted that since . . . since I was in my twenties. Since we were together. I'm happy for you, Les, but I'm not going to pretend it doesn't hurt."

"You're hurt."

"Yes. I'll get over it." She would not. "But it does sting."

"Let me ask you something, Ruth. Was I supposed to turn down the job because I'm your ex-husband, or because I'm a man?"

"I don't know. Maybe both, maybe neither. I don't begrudge you taking the job, but did you ever wonder whether it's really yours to take? If maybe there are people out there who have trained for that position, set their sights on it, busted ass to get it—only to lose it to someone who thinks it will be fun? A little hobby? It's not as if you're hurting for cash, Lester. You could have taken a breath. Another coaching offer would have come in. Any small market team would be lucky to have you."

Lester let silence swell between them. The silence, because it was under his command, imbued Lester with authority while rendering Ruth long-winded and difficult to parse. "I suppose," Lester said finally, "that in my shoes you'd have insisted the job go to someone more deserving?"

Ruth was quick to respond, "I think I might have, yeah."

"I see. But as things stand, no one is more qualified to do Ruth Devon's job than Ruth Devon herself."

Back then, he was still pronouncing her last name with a barely perceptible emphasis on the first syllable to remind Ruth the name was not hers. That she had borrowed it like a sweater and neglected to give it back.

At the time, she was still the only woman who had ever called an NBA game on national TV. Journalists writing their long-form profiles on Ruth, featuring her airbrushed headshot alongside grainy stills of her college games, loved to note that Ruth had lucked into her celebrity. What they never noted was that the kind of *luck* on which her career depended did not seem to exist for Black women, not even in basketball.

Supposedly, Ruth's field favors professionals. If you played professionally, if you coached professionally, you should have a leg up in sports media. And yet no former WNBA players or female coaches have managed to dethrone Ruth, college player from Virginia with the busted knee. Ruth might have chosen any sport— as a kid she had dominated at tennis and softball and soccer. Even golf. But she had chosen basketball, the sport that least belonged to her. To apologize would be disingenuous; Ruth has no regrets. What she could not admit to Lester then, but admits freely now, is that he was right: She would not hand over her microphone to someone more deserving. Not willingly. She could collapse courtside and, she is sure, retain her white-knuckled grip on the mic. Ruth loves her work. She is grateful for her so-called luck. Does it hurt to admit this? Does it help?

Ruth has no idea. But she remembers how desperate she was for Lester to admit the job was not his to take and he was taking it anyway. That Ruth had earned the contract, and Lester was ecstatic to be signing his name.

To his credit, Lester did seem to consider self-deprecation. At least he hesitated, oscillating between possible tactics before landing on maximum defensiveness.

"No one could ever deny that you work like a dog"—this was not a compliment—"but, truth be told, you're just not a great analyst.

You're good, okay? You're professional and knowledgeable. But you're too withholding. You never give the fans your raw, uncensored opinion, and that lack of transparency, it gets to people."

Ruth wanted to hang up. She was about to sob in an airport TGI Fridays. Fat, hot tears rolling down her cheeks, smacking against her fries. Fuming at Lester had turned her margarita buzz into a premature hangover—and wasn't the buzz yet another thing he had stolen from her?

Did Lester truly not understand why Ruth could never give her uncensored opinion on air? Did he not know that to be a woman was to censor, to measure, to calibrate? If he wanted her opinion, he could have it free of charge.

"You're a smug, condescending bastard. I hope you don't turn our daughter into the kind of person who feels entitled to everything she's ever wanted."

Lester was the one who hung up, laughing at a high and wheezy pitch.

Every former couple has the fight that follows, sometimes by years or whole decades, what they took to be the last fight. Like the kernel of corn that pops as you're tearing into the bag, the final spat bursts without warning. It comes closest to addressing the crux of all previous fights but still falls short. (Precision would mean progress, would mean hope, and Ruth never had any.) In the end, this fight served only one purpose: it allowed Ruth to hurl insults at Lester from a TGI Fridays booth. Looking back, she considers it a win.

Ruth and Lester's fame, by now, exists wholly independent of their defunct marriage. The newest generation of reporters and interns don't even register Ruth and Lester as exes. Last season, Ruth's audio assistant learned the truth of their shared surname, then shrugged and confessed, "I always figured Lester was your dad."

At the end of the first quarter the Wildcats are down twelve, and if anyone asked Ruth to account for the deficit, she would do so in defensive rotations made and missed, in fouls called or missed, in fractions of inches and seconds. Pick-and-rolls, elevator doors, box and one, give and go. Switch everything! Switch nothing! Isolation, run it back again. Glance at your popcorn and you may miss the turning point of the game. Ruth does not look away.

Of course, no one asks.

Ruth leaves her seat to meet her crew at the away team's bench. She passes beneath Cincinnati's basket, skirting the assembly of photographers sitting cross-legged on the floor. She comes close to brushing against the bony knees of Taylor Swift and her supermodel friend. With beery urgency, Taylor gestures from her black turtle-neck to Ruth's: "We're twinning!" she mouths, or shouts—there's too much noise to be sure. Ruth nods and beams at Taylor, same as she would at anyone. Later, her indifference toward the pop star will make her laugh, will make Ariana intone "OhmygodMom" in exasperation. But in this moment Taylor is the fan and Ruth is Ruth. She joins Julian, who sticks up a meaty thumb. Her A2, Simone—of the winged eyeliner, cleavage, and deadpan sense of humor—fiddles with Ruth's mic and passes it back to her.

The interview, between fifteen and twenty seconds long, will air after the next commercial break. Coach's back is turned, hands on his hips creasing his oversized suit jacket—a bad sign. You're fine, Ruth tells herself. Nerves can't show. Every word she speaks into a mic tonight is an audition. By the start of next season, she could be the analyst, free to comment on lineups, matchups, schemes, and plays from the safety of the booth.

Or she could be right here, steeling herself as she taps a famously cantankerous coach on the shoulder.

He gives his clipboard to an assistant and hunches in Ruth's direction. The question she has prepared pertains to an odd substitution Bell made midquarter: the steady veteran Anthony Moore—playing well in the opening minutes—for the inexperienced yet electric rookie Willie Glass. In her seat she tilted her head; through her IFB earpiece, she listened to Lester and Jay exchange network-friendly versions of *what the fuck*. But now she is inches from Bell's bloodshot eyes and mouth clamped lipless, and she knows the question is wrong. The man is in a mood.

Truthfully, Ruth is unbothered by Bell's frequent Grandpa-ish mourning of the league's good ole days, before defense and post play were rendered otiose by the vulgar three-point shot. Long before coaches were subjected to the in-game interview. Personally, Ruth loves the three-point shot. The collectively held breath of the arena as the ball arcs over the court, fate uncertain—she lives for that.

The coach interviews she could live without.

It should be noted that Rick Bellantoni is among the most effective coaches in the league. Head coach for almost three decades, Bell has led the Wildcats to the playoffs season after season—whether their roster has been star-studded or starved for talent. Though it makes for a less salacious narrative than the Darius Lake revenge plot, Ruth knows Bell deserves as much if not more credit for Cincinnati's success. His reputation is that of "a good man" in ways both old-school and contemporary. A veteran of the United States

Army, a devoted husband and father. A humanitarian, according to the *New Yorker*, "with a big heart and deep pockets." Ruth has seen the viral pictures of him at Black Lives Matter protests. She's gotten him on the record saying he supports any player's decision to kneel during the anthem. She's moved by his solidarity with the guys on his team, which she believes is genuine.

It must also be noted that Rick Bellantoni is a loose cannon. A quick search will yield video compilations of the man hemorrhaging rage in front of referees, assistant coaches, his own players. To Ruth's knowledge, he has never howled at a reporter, but he does nothing to hide his resentment of the network's contractual right to ask him two questions per game. At best, Bell is standoffish and annoyed, tucking in his white-stubbled chin, staring courtward and deploying as few words as possible. At worst, he looks up at you with slow-burning malice, the way a father regards a teenage daughter who has backed the family car into a telephone pole.

At the last second, Ruth changes her strategy. She abandons her question about the substitution.

"I know you have a lot on your plate tonight, Bell, so I'm only going to ask you one question. In the first quarter, what happened for your team offensively?"

The question is a freebie. From another coach, Ruth would expect an innocuous call for better execution and ball movement, plus a polite nod at the camera. But there is a reason Bell makes frequent cameos in Ruth's stress dreams. He is the TSA agent looking between Ruth's ID and her face and asking, "Is this a joke?" He is the ER doctor refusing to tell Ruth if her daughter will be okay. Or he is himself and Ruth is late to meet Joel, late to her father's funeral, late to pick her mother up from the airport because she cannot convince the man to answer a single goddamn question.

Bell takes his time peeling his gaze from the floor. With one finger he scratches his jowl. Though the arena pulses with the beat of a pop song, to which Seattle's dancers fling their limbs and spin, Ruth can hear the nail scrape against stubble. A childhood feeling washes over her: that of a Virginia Beach roller coaster lifting Ruth and her brother high above sand, sea, and their parents. Dreading the forthcoming free fall, Ruth turned to her brother and said, "I'm ready to get off now."

Bell scratches, stares. To preserve her smile, she pictures him with a martini in hand, sleeves rolled, elbows on the table. Pressure mounts behind Ruth's eyes. She won't cry. She is smiling and she won't stop until Bell relents.

Time yawns its jaws and swallows her hope. To Bell, these seconds are already a waste: might as well throw a silent fit, stage an in-game protest.

Nothing will prevent this interview from becoming a meme, but if the man cracks even the suggestion of a smile, Ruth will be in on, no longer the butt of, the joke. She holds out.

He does not smile. He doesn't even blink. Nine seconds have passed since she asked him a question.

"We're on television," Ruth reminds him. Her voice wavers.

"Ah," he says, cheeks sagging. He crinkles his eyes with a gentleman's neutered charm. Someday Ruth's cheeks will sag. Her neck will fold like an accordion and her knuckles will swell—and by the time it happens, the camera will have long forgotten her. "Lucky us."

The coach turns. His open suit jacket brushes against Ruth's fist as he moves past her.

Ruth avoids her A2's frown—which, coming from Simone, counts as sympathy—and scurries back to her home base. With trembling hands—*shit*—she hits the talk-back button on her mic and asks her producer, "Are we airing that?"

"Yup," Phillip says in the distracted tone of someone trying to merge onto the interstate.

Of course he's airing it. Why wouldn't he? Coach interviews, as a genre, are strained and hollow, impervious to real insight or emotion. Tonight, Bell gave them anger, despair, impatience! He put Ruth in her place by suggesting she stand there and absorb it all. She obliged.

The game will resume in a matter of seconds. She needs it sooner—needs the Wildcats to come back from their twelve-point deficit, needs the Sonics to feel the pressure. Needs the snap of the net, the impact of a hard pick, point guards calling out plays. Needs the game to liquefy her. Because nothing short of good basketball will drown out the echo of her own voice (did it crack with shame? Fear?) as she begged Rick Bellantoni for mercy.

We're on television.

CHAPTER SIX

When a game is in progress she has no personal life, per Ruth Devon policy. Last year an earthquake struck southern California and reverberated one-hundred and fifty miles east, rocking the Las Vegas arena where Ruth, Lester, and Jay were calling a summer league game as a trio. Ruth watched the screens on the broadcast table quiver, saw the scoreboard sway high above the court. Lester and Jay were riffing on a player from France, a point guard, tiny and lithe, with inexplicable prowess at the rim.

"Barthez with the hesitation, spin, and he finishes!" Jay marveled.

"He's a whirling dervish," Lester said.

"A French revolution is what he is," Jay said.

"Oui, oui."

Calmly, Ruth said, "We are feeling the effects of an earthquake."

"Whoa. You're right." Lester gripped Ruth's forearm.

"The ref has stopped the game. Players seem confused. Unclear whether fans will need to evacuate—I'm a little concerned about the movement of the scoreboard, not to mention the overall structure of the arena—but we will keep you updated as this event unfolds."

Her daughter was safe on the East Coast. And maybe Ruth knew as much in the core of her consciousness, or maybe she forgot she was anyone's mother. Possibly Ruth is addicted to the way her work effaces her. Losing herself in the simultaneous currents of the game and the telecast is easy from the vantage point of the booth, where she was that night. No cameras in her face. No awkward hustling from one huddle to another. Her headset snug like armor.

Tonight, Ruth's policy is failing her. Or she is failing it. Joel finally tunes into the game after the third quarter, during Ruth's uneventful interview with Sonics coach Andre Morris, as tight-lipped as Bell but politely so. *You look beautiful*, says Joel's text message. Halfway through the fourth, Ruth is still thinking about it.

She could quit. She could accept she is not going to get Lester's job. That the network executives will find a reason to keep her on the sideline, assuming the near-tears with which she gifted them tonight weren't enough on their own. Because clearly, she can't think on her feet. Or come up with a question worthy of Bell's consideration—and anyway, wasn't it unprofessional the way her lips parted and froze? The way her makeup looked, on-screen, like permanent humiliation?

She needs fresh air. A breeze to cool the sweat beading at her temples, the sharp, clarifying smell of the ocean. Something Ruth didn't foresee when she was younger was how much of her life would be spent inside. And not the comforting interior of a home or an office or a coffee shop, but the vast, commercialized spaces of stadiums and airports. Where windows don't open and you need a map to find an exit. As a kid in Hampton, Virginia she was always outdoors. If she wasn't shooting hoops at the park, she was on the beach. Ruth has promised herself that if she ever loses her job, she will move somewhere warm and coastal.

Wouldn't the West Coast be ideal? She could turn in her mic, her IFB, her notes. She could coach high school basketball and jog along the shoreline with Ariana and get a dog. A rowdy rescue of a dog, a female with soft ears and a propeller-tail, who needs to be walked first thing in the morning and schooled in obedience. Ruth would be good at training a dog. She would commit to that bitch. Ruth's heart races as she flirts with the idea, the way a person might close their eyes on the highway to flirt with death. The number of men vying for Lester's job is in the double digits. Ruth's competition played professional basketball and coached professional basketball. The job is not hers, it never was, and she ought to pull herself from the running before she is rejected.

The game gets tight. The score is tied when Wildcats point guard Denzel Kerr, as cocky as he is Christian, sinks a three from the logo and the camera catches him mouthing *motherfuckers* toward the Sonics and *thank you, Jesus* toward the rafters. Sonics ball: Kasey Powell, the former Wildcat for whom Darius was traded, sees Emory slip a pick and dive toward the rim. Emory receives the lob and dunks in one motion, shaking the backboard and, through the crowd's response, the whole arena. *Overtime*, Ruth thinks wishfully. She would take two overtimes, or three: that the game has to end at some point—that basketball is time-bound, zero-sum—is the problem.

After a stop, the Sonics have the ball with seventeen seconds left. Emory Turner is alone, dribbling down the clock at the top of the key. As the crowd's roar rises to the decibel that lodges in your chest and splits open your ears, Powell sets a screen. And there's the switch: Turner is staring down Darius Lake. Turner crosses over, steps back, crosses over again; these moves would usually leave his defender off balance and grasping as Emory shoots over him or blows by him. Tonight, Emory's defender is the one person who can read his mind.

Ruth, who prefers to keep her eyes on live action, happens to glance at her monitor in time to catch a close shot of Lake's face, his upper lip curling: Is he talking trash on the game's final possession? What did he say? Ruth hits the talk-back button reflexively. "What did he say?" She might as well be screaming into the surf.

Too much time has passed. Emory's only choice is to take a one-legged fadeaway from twenty feet with Darius draped all over him. It's a prayer, a brick. The buzzer is the crowd's heart flatlining.

Ruth will never quit this job. She would sooner be dragged from the court.

In Ruth's ear, and on televisions across America, Jay Thomas concludes, "It could have been a game-winner, but Turner's shot is no good—and Game One goes to the Wildcats."

Ruth is rising, telling Phillip she wants Darius for the walk-out ("No shit" is his staticky reply) when she and Lester lock eyes across the floor.

He is shoulder to shoulder with Jay in the booth, his features framed by his headset, his traffic-cone-orange tie muted by the bedlam of the court. Lester's expression cracks open, as if locating Ruth amid the throngs of Times Square or an airport terminal. Ruth considers his vasectomy. The chilling implications of it. After their divorce, Lester cut his losses, closed up shop? She hadn't known.

And a surge of nausea—at the thought of the scalpel? Or else
Lester's loyalty—makes Ruth wish he had never told her.

An NBA game overwhelms the senses. It's not the optics or the
forced bodily contact but the acoustics, the deluge of sound, that
can throw Ruth off balance if she's not careful. She has watched
walkout interviews after Wimbledon, one voice at a time echoing
in a tennis club, hushed, church-like—the assignment would be
as alien to Ruth as a gig on the moon. In her ear, Phillip is saying
she has a full minute to talk to Darius. Julian gestures for her to
move closer to the player. Behind Ruth, two assistant coaches are
shouting civilities at each other. Intermittent and alarming are
the shrieks of dispersing fans; constant is the rumble of those still
seated; and threatening to drown it all out is the arena's house
music, blaring through the ceiling-mounted speakers, throbbing
at the base of Ruth's skull.

She leans into Darius. On more than one occasion Ruth has
been asked to rank the smelliest players in the league. She won't
do it, but she will tell you who, after a forty-eight-minute game,
smells inexplicably like soap and fresh apples.

That would be Darius Lake.

"You're certainly known as a two-way player, but in the second
half tonight you exceeded expectations on the defensive end. Can
you tell us what was going through your mind as you guarded
Emory Turner on that last play?"

She's hollering. The background noise will be adjusted for
the broadcast, and in the absence of interference Ruth will sound
unhinged. Men will take to Reddit: *Why is Ruth Devon's voice so*

strained? Why is she always screaming at everyone like my lesbian gym teacher in 1993?

"Um." Darius hunches toward her, smoothing his braids with a flattened palm. "I saw what he was up to, and I thought I'd shut it down." He speaks without inflection, in a voice so deep and tranquilizing Ruth can imagine the expedience with which he lulled his newborn babies to sleep.

"This has to be an emotionally challenging series for you. You and Emory Turner were the faces of the franchise here in Seattle for the better part of a decade. Seattle's offense set screen after screen, forcing you to defend your former teammate, and you didn't lose your composure, not for a moment. But it's only Game One. Where do you go from here?"

"I usually go back to the hotel after the game."

Ruth smiles, waiting him out. Playing with fire on live television. Again.

"Unless it's a home game," he clarifies. "Then I go home."

Ruth says, "Let me rephrase: How is your team feeling heading into Game Two?"

"We plan to win it."

Ruth chuckles her segment-ending chuckle. "You steal two games on the road, I think you'll make a lot of people back home very happy." She's about to thank him when he stoops toward the microphone.

"What about you? Would you be happy?"

Both reporting and basketball are games of split-second reactions. Ruth's subject can thwart her plans as easily as a well-executed defense. Certain players love to tease her, throwing questions back in her face; from Emory Turner she would expect this. Prepare for it, even. Heading into the interview with Darius Lake, Ruth doubted she could keep him on air for a full minute. Since when is he playful? When has he ever been coy?

When a player offers the media something it hasn't seen before, the most common mistake is to pretend nothing happened. To filter out responses that don't conform to a preconceived impression. When, in these moments of uncertainty, the reporter pauses instead? She gets gold.

Ruth tilts her head and looks at Darius openly. "Where there's basketball, I'm always happy," she says.

He extends a palm, requesting hers. Ruth shifts the mic from her right hand to her left, allowing Darius Lake to dap her up on live television. In the production truck, her director will shout, "Stay with Ruth. Stay . . . stay . . ." Milking the moment. Savoring the debut of a more confident, candid Darius Lake—finally freed from his function as Emory's foil. Ruth imagines, with a mixture of relief and apprehension, the clip obliterating tonight's interview with Rick Bellantoni, burying the coach a thousand thumbnails deep.

"Thank you, Darius."

"Thanks, Ruth." He turns away from the camera, peeling off his jersey to give to his mom, who is making her way down the concrete steps.

Ruth exhales on "Jay," tossing back to the booth, as she must.

CHAPTER SEVEN

In her hotel room Ruth scrubs her face clean. She knots her hair and slips into one of several university-branded hoodies she collected discretely on last year's college tour with Ariana. (The idea was to present her daughter with the pertinent hoodie as soon as Ariana chose a school; alas, the hoodies were absorbed by Ruth's collection of athleisure wear.) Comfortable, Ruth can no longer access the body-based anxiety that creeps up on her before each broadcast, Angie laboring over Ruth's face like a conservator intent on restoring some neglected work of art.

When she was younger, Ruth was virtuously unvain. Her bowl cuts grew into incidental mullets. Her knees were scarred, if not actively bleeding. She wore prescription athletic goggles, purchased begrudgingly by Cheryl after Ruth smashed two pairs of glasses on the basketball court. Then came college, her crush on Coach Devon followed by a career on television. Ever since: a mental map, its topography detailed, of her physical imperfections. For a long time the combination of professional makeup artists and Ruth's workout routine kept her conventionally beautiful. She has thick blond hair, bright eyes, and a round nose of the kind popularized by Y2K-era actresses whom magazines described as "girls next door." Then Ruth got older and her metabolism slowed, softened her chin and dimpled her arms. Her hard work etched itself into the fragile skin around her eyes. There was a time in her late-thirties when she kept expecting to wake up with her beauty refreshed, as if emerging from an illness or a particularly brutal hangover. When it dawned on her that the wrinkles were permanent, she was more fascinated than bereft: so *this* is what I look like.

Her age answered questions. About money (fifty cents to Lester's dollar—still plenty) and marriage (nope) and children (just the one). It took time, but eventually she settled into these answers the way you settle into a new house or haircut. It is mostly a relief to be forty-two. To the extent that her job pressures her to chase both the appearance and the mindset of a younger woman, it's pressure she resents. To the extent that Joel has ripped open the seams of the answered questions, Ruth feels a slow-seeping panic. She half-wishes she could drop to one knee and ask Joel to be her boyfriend indefinitely. Never leaving, forever not her husband. That could be sweet, right?

Or devastating.

Lounging in bed, sipping conservatively but also directly from the bottle of whiskey Joel ordered to her room while she was gone, Ruth relives her night.

> This is insane. Literally the most @dariuslake has ever said at once.

> OMFG did @dariuslake just do a JOKE? On the TELEVISION?

> Go home, Darius. You're drunk.

> @dariuslake out here trying so damn hard to be Emory, like that'll get him the dub. Smdh.

> Normalize @dariuslake making facial expressions.

> @dariuslake flirting with @HeyRD. Big mood, bro.

> Lol @dariuslake trying to get Ruth to admit she's rooting for Seattle.

> Ahhhh don't think I've ever seen @HeyRD speechless. Well played, sir.

Surprised to learn Darius has a Twitter account, Ruth taps his avatar. In the last decade he has tweeted twice. Once to share a heavily hashtagged picture of himself playing mini golf, and again, several years later, to congratulate Serena Williams on her twenty-second grand slam.

She is still scrolling, lying flat on the bed in her bra and shapewear, when Twitter goes dark to accommodate an incoming call from Phillip.

"That interview," he says without preamble. Ruth last saw Phillip in the parking lot outside the production truck. An intern was filming him with a phone, asking, "Who on your staff would you say is indispensable?" Phillip pulled Ruth into his arms. "This lady. Always this lady."

Now Phillip says, "That was wild. What was that?"

"I guess he was feeling good."

"That was the most he's ever said at one time!"

All the same tweets have leapt to the top of Phillip's feed. Ruth says, "Look, no one expected the Wildcats to make it this far. As a comeback story, it's irresistible. He's not immune to that."

There's a pause. It's hard to imagine Phillip without an energy drink or iced coffee in hand. At one in the morning he must be swigging from something else. Scotch. Or NyQuil.

"You think he got jealous of your friendship with Turner?"

"I wouldn't say I have a friendship with Turner."

"You two have a rapport. It's no secret. On media day you were looking extremely friendly."

A text message dings loudly in her ear. She suspects Lester but waits to check. "We're friend-*ly*, sure. We're not friends. Look, I have no idea what's gotten into Darius, but I can tell you I'm here for it. Bell, on the other hand . . ."

"Oh, don't worry about Bell. He's a cranky old man. Everyone knows that."

"Casual fans don't know that. They're watching and thinking, 'Wow, this guy hates her guts.'"

"Everyone in the truck gets it. Everyone at the network gets it."

Ruth takes a breath and braces herself. "I don't know if they've made any decisions about next season, but I feel like I didn't do myself any favors tonight."

Phillip sounds suddenly, conveniently distracted, opting for a variation on what he's already said. "His team was down twelve. When the deficit goes over ten, Bell gets his panties in a twist. Hardly your fault."

Ruth's stomach churns. She hasn't eaten since before the game.

"I wasn't prepared. I should have been faster to fill the silence. Or cut the interview short. Anything."

"Ruth, don't stress about this. What I can promise you, with absolute certainty, is that we're bringing you back next season. Maybe not as an analyst, maybe on the sideline again. Bottom line is: nothing that happened tonight is going to threaten your role as a reporter. Got it?"

Ruth hears a groan, as if Phillip has pulled a muscle in his neck or let a beverage slip from his hand. Ruth assumes Phillip is alone in his hotel room, ice cubes now melting into the woven Pendleton rug. The furniture draped in suit jackets and ties; the nightstand crowded with cups and the punctured aluminum packaging of allergy medication. His wife, ten years younger, has stopped joining him on the road since the birth of their twins. When it comes to marriages that feature wide, treacherous age gaps, Ruth tries but can't withhold judgment. She no longer believes age is only a number denoting trips around the sun. Or that it was an accident of timing, Ruth being born thirteen rotations after Lester. What she does believe is that a man who spent his youth doting on his career—or, maybe, doting on nothing and no one—searches deliberately for a younger woman. Because if you're a straight man, what difference is there between thirty and marrying thirty? A woman's fertility, her time, her energy—it's all yours for the taking.

Ruth takes a breath. "I just want to reiterate . . . I'm committed to being a full-time analyst. I know it's a huge step, but I'm ready for it."

Phillip says nothing. Ruth is sure her assertions have rankled him. She is supposed to be casual, not so desperate. She is supposed to chill out.

"Ruth?" In the few seconds of silence Phillip has shed his authority and closed the space between them. His warmth proves he is on her side, and also the existence of an opposing side. Some forgone conclusion he has so far resisted. "All I can say is, if you don't get the job? It won't be because you don't deserve it."

Ruth thanks him, as if he has told her something she doesn't already know.

The text says

> Room service? I'm in 708.

Ruth slides her phone beneath the covers and doesn't reply. She's cozy. The whiskey has cut through the adrenaline that kept her heart slamming long after the buzzer. Instead of responding to Lester she sends Joel a heart emoji, which he won't see until morning. She would like to text Ariana a whole screenful of hearts but refrains. There exists a precise volume of communication to which Ariana will respond willingly. One emoji too many yields crushing silence.

Ruth tries to sleep. The Juniper Seattle is a historic building, close to the market with views of the Sound and (on sunny days, it is rumored) Mt. Rainer. The floors are the original polished oak, the beds made as smooth as a just-opened jar of peanut butter. But her room's temperature is governed by a gaping vent above the window: at irregular intervals the vent roars to life, bellows hoarsely, and finishes with a demoralized sigh. No matter how many nights Ruth spends here, she always forgets the vent shortly after check-out, only to become reacquainted with it during her next stay as she tosses and turns, gets up to pee, lies in the dark scrolling, scrolling.

She opens Ariana's Instagram. This feels okay, at first. The photos are airbrushed, her daughter's posture so stiff and unnatural that Ruth can almost dismiss the images as fiction. A fantasy. The pictures are someone's interpretation of sex, sure—a bra strap sliding down a shoulder, a sweater riding up to reveal painted-on abdominal muscles—but to Ruth, who knows what her daughter looks like slumped in a passenger seat or inhaling a burrito, it all seems staged. Ruth's primary emotion is secondhand embarrassment, same as when a younger Ari was obsessed with emulating the canned vocals and half-hearted gyrations of certain pop stars.

Now Ruth is zooming in on a picture of Ariana kneeling in the foamy sheets of the Atlantic at low tide. Knees far apart. One hand dangling over a breadstick thigh, the other touching her own face. When was this taken? The photography looks professional, yet no one bothered to erase the bean-shaped birthmark from Ariana's left hip.

The birthmark was the first thing Ruth knew about her daughter.

She sends the link to Roxanne Phalen, senior sportswriter and Ruth's closest friend at the network. Somewhere in the hotel Roxanne reclines on a bed identical to Ruth's, maybe cyber-stalking her own teenage daughters, all of them sweetly stout and at no risk of being scouted as they lounge poolside in tankinis, giggling beneath heavy bangs. Frequently Roxanne acts as a vessel for Ruth's surplus of anxiety, always ready to cringe, clutch her diastasis recti, and moan in sympathy. That Roxanne can't keep a secret does not matter in this context, Ariana having opted to bare all.

> Pretty girl

Roxanne replies.

Ruth

I hate this.

Roxanne

Of course you do!! She looks
THIN. Is she eating?!

Ruth

Like a horse when we're together.
I guess that's her natural figure—
Lester's mom was always slender.
It would kill me if she had an
eating disorder.

Roxanne

I'm sure she doesn't. If there's one
thing she got from you, it's that
CONFIDENCE. 💪 Is someone
looking out for her during these
shoots? Her agent?

Ruth

I don't know.

Roxanne

Is she enjoying it?

Ruth

I don't know.

Roxanne

😬 Try to get some sleep, Mama.

Ruth is no longer committed to sleep. She is rising from the bed and sliding her bare feet into Nikes. In room 708, Lester will have an Ambien for her. And maybe, if she's transparent with him, information about her contract. But certainly the Ambien.

She does not reply to his message—though there's another one now:

Where are you?

Not replying is an unnecessary precaution; Joel doesn't snoop through Ruth's inbox. The guy is almost pathologically non-jealous. Granted, in describing her bygone marriage, Ruth tends to emphasize past conflicts and downplay her lingering affection for Lester. A divorcée's prerogative. It has occurred to her that Joel might view her, or Les, as fundamentally depleted, lacking the spark to charge even late-night room service with sexual tension. But that can't be right: Joel once informed Ruth that her fondness for hotel sex qualifies as a fetish. And no one imagines Lester Devon immune to the newest generation of sideline reporters, all of whom have correctly intuited that the uniform includes cleavage, never dabbling, as Ruth did, in androgynous business wear.

Another possibility is that Joel underestimates the number of hours Ruth logs with her ex. Between pressers and greenrooms and airport lounges and hotel lobbies, Lester is Ruth's most constant companion. She neither hides this reality from Joel nor paints him a picture. If he watched the games, or typed her name into a search bar, or pressed her for the details of her days, he would already know.

Ruth leaves her phone charging on the nightstand and takes the whiskey. She steps into the brightness of the deserted hallway. Room 708 is seven floors down, directly beneath hers. The elevator doors slide open with an indiscreet *ding*.

The elevator is not empty. Against the mirrored wall slumps Emory Turner, one enormous hand buried in his curls, the other cupped around his phone. Between the conference finals and media day, Emory went to the barber; Ruth has already noted the clean edges of his signature low fade. Distracted by his strength and his size—during his rookie season, Emory, still a teenager, grew a final two inches—journalists rarely observe that the man is classically beautiful. That his Black skin is baby-smooth, practically poreless, or that his smile evokes crisp suits and red carpets.

Ruth exclaims his name with high-pitched girlish delight—her voice, in this moment, unaltered since high school. Annoyance creases Emory's forehead as he moves to stall the elevator doors. "You going down?" he asks.

Ruth is frozen. With confusion, because Emory Turner does not seem to recognize her. With self-consciousness, because if he does recognize her, she is wearing leggings and no makeup and carrying an open bottle of liquor by the neck. And with alarm, because Emory Turner should not be here. He lives in Seattle with his wife and two girls. To step foot inside the Juniper tonight is to cross enemy lines. It's reckless; anyone could see him and snap a picture and set rumors aflame: Emory Turner is blackmailing Darius Lake into losing the finals on purpose. Emory Turner is having an affair with a Wildcats PR assistant. Emory Turner is taking clandestine meetings with Cincinnati's front office in advance of his free agency.

Emory's features are strained with impatience. He repeats his question.

Ruth has heard that women in their forties are invisible. A woman her age could kidnap a child, shoplift a Le Creuset dutch oven, or spit on a cop, and witnesses would disbelieve their own eyes. Ruth, being famous, being primped and pampered and televised, has neither enjoyed this phenomenon nor withered as a result of it. Maybe occasionally, pushing a shopping cart through the aisles of Target at 8:00 a.m. on a Wednesday, her yoga pants and ponytail the uniform of suburban motherhood, she has felt youthful eyes measuring her as they would an upcoming pothole in the road, registering not a woman but a certain amount of space to be avoided. More often, people see her and whisper—or stutter or scream—her name.

Now she feels it, the invisibility. Emory Turner is looking through her. Ruth has had dinner with his wife. She has held his daughter and laughed when the infant rooted against the silk folds of her blouse. In locker rooms she has seen Emory in nothing but a towel held noncommittally around his waist. If she's being honest, she has seen him without the towel too, though she always looks up, up toward the impossible height of his shoulders, his jaw. Because she is a professional. And a prude.

The man who described Ruth Devon as the GOAT on national television is staring into the hallway, seeing only the inconvenience of an awestruck fan.

"No," Ruth says. "You go ahead."

Emory nods and steps back. Standing straight, his head nearly collides with the elevator's ceiling. As the doors slide shut Ruth thinks she sees a change in his expression—a spark of recognition, a surge of regret. This could be wishful thinking.

Ruth is tempted to tell Roxanne about the sighting. Roxanne has been working on a piece analyzing the effects of the season's biggest trade deal, and she's hungry for the kind of details that braid each player's performance with his personal life. But without knowing what Turner was doing in the Wildcats' hotel, the detail would be merely intriguing. And if Emory did, after all, recognize Ruth standing dumbly in the hall, he would know who outed him. What the players think of her concerns Ruth more than it does Roxanne. In part because Ruth interacts with them on television, in emotional moments when most men struggle to mask their true feelings. And in part because she wants them to like her the way she likes them.

Ruth waits a moment before pressing the button, ensuring the elevator unloads its passenger before returning. By the time she hears the whir of the elevator's ascent, she has changed her mind. The tips of her ears feel hot. She is suddenly, profoundly tired—and certain that Lester has nothing she needs.

GAME TWO

Seattle, Washington

WILDCATS – SUPERSONICS

1-0

CHAPTER EIGHT

At the beginning of the second quarter Ruth becomes aware of the heat. At first she thinks she is imagining it. She often breaks a sweat on the sideline—stress, shapewear—and although this is the third in a string of unusually warm nights in Seattle, the temperature in the arena should be perfectly calibrated. But perspiration gleams on players' chests, soaking their jerseys translucent. Fans fan themselves with bent programs, groans of discomfort rolling like thunder over the stands as people peel off their complimentary Space Needle–branded T-shirts.

Phillip's voice crackles through Ruth's IFB: "I'm getting reports that the AC is down in the arena. Can you confirm?"

Minutes ago the Wildcats were up five. Now they are down three. Darius Lake misses a jump shot and lands clutching his left calf. He's hopping, mouthing something to Anthony Moore on the bench. Darius has been mic'ed for the game; whatever he said will soon make headlines.

"There's no air in here," Ruth confirms. "What did Lake just say?"

From the cool of the production truck, Phillip answers, "'They're trying to smoke us out of here.'"

"I'm going to figure this out."

"Yeah, you are," Phillip says. More than an order, it's a vote of confidence.

Ruth leaves her seat and speed-walks into the tunnel, smiling but ignoring the cries of her name, the phones stretched over the railing in solicitation of selfies. She intercepts Linda Zhang, Seattle's VP of communications, who has already shed her blazer and rolled up her sleeves. Linda continues toward the court, avoiding Ruth as assiduously as Ruth avoided her own fans. "Any idea what's up with the AC?" Ruth shouts as Zhang flees. "Not a good time," Zhang calls over her shoulder. "If you give me a minute—"

"Don't have a minute," Ruth says. She is already flagging down Charlie the security guard, a man with the dimensions of a refrigerator, whose mutton chops almost conceal his chubby cheeks. The two of them have often talked as Ruth waits to be let onto the court during shootaround. Charlie is a former marine who loves fly fishing, cars, and the NFL; Ruth is reasonably versed in all three. Mopping his brow with a napkin, Charlie agrees it's hot. His keycard opens a series of metal doors as he escorts Ruth to a far-flung maintenance office. Through her earpiece Ruth can hear Lester talking about Darius Lake's muscle cramps. Willie Glass is taking a free throw, and Lake is waiting on the other end of the court, fingers laced through the net, preserving energy.

The door to the maintenance office is cracked open. As Charlie raps on the frame Ruth pushes through and introduces herself to the men inside. "Ruth Devon. Wondering if I could get an update on the AC blowout. What's happening?"

Two men look up from a shared desk buried in energy drink

cans and clipboards. A roll of brown paper towels unravels toward the floor. One man takes his time adjusting to Ruth's presence, overwhelmed by her efficient tone. But the younger of the two jumps to his feet, mouth ajar. "Oh my God. Shit. Hi."

Ruth waits. To balance out his reaction, he will now err on the side of overly casual. He'll call her by her first name, ask her how she's been.

"Ruth. How—how's it going?"

"Great. Just wondering what's up with the AC."

The kid's boss, a white man with a sallow, asymmetrical face, leans back and strains the spine of his swivel chair. "Something's fucked with the electrical system. Our guys are taking a look now. There'll be an announcement when we sort things out."

Ruth lifts an eyebrow. Charlie the security guard has already deserted her, and she is the only woman in a room so dim and airless the vibe is more bunker than office. With one ear she's listening to Lester explain that Darius Lake is asking to be taken out of the game. In moments of bewilderment Lester's voice takes on a vulnerable, childlike quality. Ruth thinks of the text on her phone from three nights ago, which she never answered and which they have not discussed.

> Where are you?

The message evokes one hundred voicemails left on cubic Nokia cell phones. To read it is to succumb to a wave of phantom panic: All these years on the road, has Lester been trapped at home with Ariana? Pouring too-hot bathwater over their daughter's head and forgetting to brush her teeth? No. She owes Lester nothing—nothing, that is, except a read on the temperature in the arena.

"You're kidding," she says. "It must be ninety degrees on the court. The players are in pain. Some communication from the building would be appreciated."

A sneer lifts one corner of the boss's mustache. "Try to stay calm. You'll have your answers by the time your article's due."

"I'm not writing an article." Ruth speaks slowly now, her conde-scension masquerading as patience. "I'm reporting from the sideline of Game Two of the NBA finals. Which is happening now. In this arena. Right now."

"Dude," hisses the kid. "She's Ruth Devon."

"Well, I guess we better let *Ruth Devon* get back to the game." The man says her name like it's a bullshit alias. Jane Doe. What's-her-face.

Ruth looks to the kid, giving him a chance to counter-offer. Is his eyebrow ring uncomfortable? Ruth didn't think to get her ears pierced until she was in her late twenties, when Lester inexplicably gave her a pair of gold hoops for her birthday.

"I'm sorry," the kid says, defeated.

Ruth waves him off. She understands, intellectually, that main-tenance staff are not required to invest their hearts in the NBA finals. Their job is the same whether the arena hosts a basketball game or a sold-out Beyoncé show. But on a personal level, the indif-ference offends her. Darius Lake is sitting out the last seven minutes of the second quarter; Cincinnati is down ten. A malfunctioning circuit breaker has the power to alter the course of the finals, and it is Ruth's near-religious belief that anyone who does not care should be ejected from the building.

As she emerges from the office into the hall, her body antici-pates the relief of manufactured cold. There is none. The humidity fogs Ruth's glasses. She leans against a cinder block wall and takes a breath. She needs to return to the court for her interview with Supersonics coach Andre Morris. She trusts him not to snap, not to sabotage a telecast with nine full seconds of dead air, but that doesn't mean she knows what to expect. His team is up, sure, but he's also sweating through a ten-thousand-dollar suit. She has seen coaches unravel over less.

Ruth is from Virginia, grew up in a two-bedroom prefab without central air. On July nights she would return from the park, leave her cut-offs and Swatch watch and FRANKIE SAYS RELAX T-shirt in a heap on the bathroom floor, and stand beneath the coldest spray the shower could produce until her mother invoked the water bill. She is intimately familiar with the heat. Over the past three days in Seattle, as the temperature rose and news anchors reveled in record-breaking highs, Ruth barely registered the weather. En route from the hotel lobby to the cab, the cab to the arena, the arena to the production truck, she felt the warm air embrace her like an old friend.

In the arena, the same temperature feels lethal.

Ruth sometimes wonders if her work will be what kills her. If she'll be trampled during an emergency evacuation. Caught in the underbelly of a California stadium when the big one hits. Players fear the fans, with their purchased proximity to the court. They fear the man who stabbed Monica Seles midmatch, the thieves who ransack the homes of football players on Sundays. In Ruth's mind the predator is always the arena itself, whose vastness, meant to approximate the outdoors, keeps its occupants at an unnatural distance from the natural world. How hard would it be to escape, everyone scrambling for the exits at once?

Ruth adds heatstroke to the list of insulated dangers. A wave of vertigo causes her to brace herself against the wall. Is the building moving? The building is not moving; her phone is buzzing in her skirt pocket. Her daughter has texted her:

> Download a temp app!!!

Ruth peers down the length of the hall, confused by Ariana's omniscience. She sends back a trio of question marks and, lightning-fast, Ariana explains:

> Dad says they're waiting for you
> to report on the temperature.
> Download an app. Your phone has a
> thermometer.

It takes Ruth a second to process: what comes from the mouth of color analyst Lester Devon is, to Ariana, what "Dad says." This is a family operation. Frantically, Ruth tries to write *genius daughter* but her phone autocorrects to *genius squirrel* and there is no time to clarify. The app is downloading. Ruth is rushing back to the court, sweating off her makeup and hating her shoes. When she undresses tonight, the insoles will be stained with blood.

At the mouth of the tunnel she sidesteps a cluster of rumpled, dehydrating journalists, getting as far onto the playing surface as she can with the game still in progress. She crouches at the corner of the court, holding her phone over the waxed wood. The numbers on her screen rise as the numbers on the game clock dwindle.

It is over ninety degrees. Ruth knew it was over ninety degrees. She could tell by the sweat pooling between her breasts and the prickling at the backs of her knees. But pooling and prickling cannot be quantified; pooling and prickling amount to speculation, and Ruth does not speculate.

She returns to her home base. Hitting the talk-back button as she slides into her seat, she says, "I've got a read on the temp." Without asking for her source, Phillip communicates to the booth that Ruth is about to interrupt.

Lester, in Ruth's ear: "And here's Ruth Devon with an update from the sideline."

Ruth, trusting her mic has been opened: "The Wildcats are not the only ones feeling the heat here in Seattle tonight. Due to some kind of electrical failure, the AC is out and it is ninety-one degrees on the court."

Lester thanks her and launches into an analysis of how the heat could affect the final score. The Sonics, as a team, have more experience performing in high temperatures. Their point guard played a year in France, where stadiums are rarely air conditioned. Their Argentinian power forward doesn't appear to have noticed the climate change, while their guard from the Virgin Islands looks, in Lester's words, "invigorated."

Hailing disproportionately from the northern half of America, the Wildcats are, by contrast, hot. Their eyes are glazed, their faces dewy and flushed, expressions wilting in disbelief. And then there's Darius Lake, who is more than hot: he has a well-known tendency to cramp up. With the arena transformed into a steam room, he can barely walk.

By halftime Cincinnati is down fifteen. Wildcats retreat to the bench. They hunch their shoulders as trainers drape ice packs over their necks. The public address system blasts the hook from Nelly's "Hot in Herre," a song Ariana heard and memorized at an inappropriately young age. Ruth laughs, and to her own ear her laughter sounds hollow—a cover for her mounting anxiety. The dread that sometimes wakes her in the middle of the night, recasting the basic facts of her life as insurmountable challenges. Her palms are slicker than they ought to be, her lower back enduring a succession of sharp, shooting pains. In her quest for the exact temperature she covered miles of the stadium's underground labyrinth. She could use an ice pack, or a Gatorade.

Ruth remembers loading a two-year-old Ariana into her car seat during the swampy DC summer. How Ariana would wrinkle her small face and ask Ruth, "Ish hot? Ish hot?"

Ish hot, baby.

Ruth fishes her phone from her pocket and thanks her daughter for the tip. Ariana, wherever she is, whatever she's doing, sends Ruth a row of squirrel emoji, plus the words, *I got you.*

CHAPTER NINE

Ruth is ready to follow the home team into the tunnel, but as she stands she becomes suddenly and irreversibly conscious of the smell. Of rubber and liquefied butter and sweat.

Of the flesh-toned water that pools between hotdogs in their plastic sleeves.

Of sockless feet in grass-damp shoes.

She looks to the crowd, expecting to see faces twisted in repulsion, noses pinched shut, but no one is reacting. It's an emergency, this smell. Ruth scans the cluttered media table for an empty cup or paper bag. Finding nothing, she buries her nose in the skin of her forearm. Inhales her own sweat and soap. She's fine. The heat may be coaxing certain odors to the surface, but the truth is that the arena always smells this way. And she likes the smell, how it suffuses every game no matter the city or series. No matter the season. The smell is nostalgic and urgent and has never bothered her. She's fine—so why is she, with one hand splayed across her midsection, making her way to the booth? Stepping over photographers, circumventing stuntmen and dancers with their pompoms drooping in the heat, creeping along the perimeter, seeking out Lester.

As she approaches the booth Lester rises from his chair. "Yo," he says. "Are you okay?"

Jay stays seated, his headset slung around his neck. They are both looking at her like she has two heads. Joke's on them: theirs are the faces that won't quite focus, blurring at the edges. She might have put on someone else's glasses by mistake. Ruth pulls the frames from her face to check. The frames are red, the lenses thick, hers. To forestall panic, she polishes the lenses with the edge of her blouse.

That smell. A pipe has burst, or a long-dead body is festering somewhere in the stands. The heat has revealed the essential rot of the arena. This is not the smell of basketball. The realization comforts her.

"You smell that, right?" she asks Lester.

"Smell what? Ruth, drink some water. You look terrible."

"Thanks."

"You look like the recipient of bad news. You look like you got traded to TNT."

Ruth clamps a hand over her mouth as her stomach revolts. Was the nausea this violent last time? She banishes the thought. People get sick. Food poisoning happens.

"I'm sick," she announces, and she turns on her heel, tunnel-bound. The cinder block hallways are stuffed with reporters and interns and thin-lipped coaches. Physical therapists slinging buckets of ice. Ruth shoulders sideways through the tangle of them, wishing she was alone, at home, to contend with what she almost knows or is about to know or would rather not know. Not at work. Not at halftime. At home, at least, the bathroom floor grit rubbing against her knees would be less offensive—attributable to her own hair, own fingernails. Dirt spread by the soles of her own feet. There would be no stall door, which she has no time to lock, falling open to collide with her arched spine. The smell belching forth from the toilet bowl as she lifts the seat would be lemony Lysol, courtesy of her cleaning lady, not this atrocious decaying pipe-ammonia stench. Rust and dried urine if not for which this maybe wouldn't happen. Ruth would maybe cough and heave before resting her head in her arms.

The stench is the cue her stomach needs to eject its contents. Throat burning and eyes watering themselves blind. A powerful urge to sob. Yes, it was like this last time. She remembers, though she's convinced it was a different body that coursed with foreign hormones. That became sick and thin then round and flushed. That contracted and tore open and produced a perfect baby girl.

And it was a different body that fucked Lester Devon—the last time and the first time and all the times in between. A different body that flew upward for a layup and landed in a ruptured heap. The body Ruth has now wobbles where it once flexed, is predictable and reliable if a bit stiff. Her body belongs to no team and is home to no one but herself. Ruth was certain she had been restored to the physical autonomy of mid-childhood, which was why she'd had her IUD removed at her last appointment—or she was somewhat shy of certain, which was also why.

For the remainder of the finals, the two arenas will smell like meaty, floral death—and there will be nothing she can do except chew gum and avoid breathing.

"Have you been pregnant before?" a doctor will ask.

"Once," Ruth will say. "A long time ago."

The bathroom she chose is remote, serviced by maintenance staff infrequently. Warped mirrors shudder beneath pale, buzzing lights. In Ruth's backpack is a collection of individually wrapped breath mints, collected from restaurants and hotel lobbies—but her backpack is in a locker on the other side of the arena. What she needs more than a Lifesaver is a bottle of water. The water would slide cool and clarifying down her throat, pooling beneath the arch of her ribcage. She imagines it. The fantasy helps.

Ruth's hands stop shaking; the sirens in her head cease. She doesn't know for sure. The heat may have corrupted her senses, induced misleadingly familiar symptoms. Sure, there have been other signs: persistent cramps, an aching lower back. But she's forty-two. She could have a cyst in her uterus or chronic vertigo or the flu. Her butt could be expanding on account of age and airport dinners. That one fried chicken place in Memphis, from which her crew always orders breakdown dinner after Grizzlies games. Ruth still has the appetite of a teenage boy.

She loves a succinct explanation—no doubt, pregnancy can explain most any symptom. But she knows better than to jump to conclusions.

She's glad no one has followed her into the bathroom. Simone would have widened her eyes and deadpanned "Well, shit." Roxanne would have pressed her hands to her cheeks and bubbled over with congratulations. Ruth refuses to consider what Lester would have done. The memory of stumbling up to the pair of male broadcasters mortifies her, but vaguely, like something she did a long time ago. Not a mistake she'll repeat. She will tell Jay and Lester that she ate something bad; she's fine now.

Her face needs a touch-up. She will tell Angie nothing.

Ruth checks and, yes, she has time to duck into the green-room for a bottle of water before the start of the third quarter. The ghost of nausea is already yielding to fresh nausea. Her last bout of morning sickness lasted four months. She spent those days belly-down on the couch, head angled toward the bunny-eared television that showed only daytime talk shows and low-budget soap operas because it was the nineties. No Netflix. And no Netflix now, no couch, because she is Ruth Devon and this is Game Two of the NBA finals. She's fucked, she's completely fucked. And yet.

The fanfare of halftime reaches her through the tunnel. A thumping bassline and the stadium announcer's *ooh*s and *ah*s, muffled as if through a cup pressed against the wall. Unicyclists are dunking on each other, or an acrobat is balancing plates atop her head, or a dog is donning sunglasses and hopping on a skateboard, carving up the floor like a Venice Beach legend. Twenty-four minutes of regulation remain. It's miserable in the arena tonight, but the misery—its strange source, its surreal temperature—is unprecedented. People will be talking about this game for decades. Try as she might, Ruth can't think of a single place she'd rather be.

Darius Lake sits out the entirety of the third quarter.

By the time Ruth is in place for her interview with Coach Morris she has sweat off her makeup. She has raked her meticulously styled hair into a ponytail and pushed her silky sleeves to her elbows. "You look great," says Julian, pit stains overtaking his T-shirt. "Like you're on vacation."

Ruth laughs. "Hey, people pay good money to sweat like this."

Coach Andre Morris radiates camera-ready joy. A former point guard for the Atlanta Hawks, Andre is one of seven Black coaches across a league of thirty-two teams. In the late eighties, a picture of him mean-mugging, torn from the pages of *Sports Illustrated*, had a place of honor on Ruth's bedroom wall between Kareem and Jordan. Halfway through Ruth's first season with the network, when she was thirty-one and freshly divorced, Andre's third wife brought their six-month-old daughter to a game. Ruth gathered the baby in her arms and instead of thinking *I'm holding Andre Morris's baby*, she thought *I'm holding a baby.*

Since the end of halftime, Ruth's spirits have been bolstered by the possibility—slight, though intoxicating—that being pregnant is no problem. Is fine or even good. The idea came to her as welcome as daybreak after a bad dream and now she can't let it go. She has a boyfriend. A young and able-bodied, family-friendly boyfriend who wants to marry her. Joel is so desperate to marry her he predicted this development, didn't he? Over expensive, oddly-colored pasta he said they could have a baby. Or talk about having a baby. Or talk about talking about having a baby. Joel said the word *baby*, Ruth is certain.

Coach is grinning at her. It's the way players sometimes grin during their walkout interviews after scoring the game-winner. Ruth smiles back, a little bit starstruck. Around Andre she often is.

"How's your team coping with the heat?" Ruth asks.

"Oh, they're holding up great. Some extra sweat isn't going to take down a group like this. Is it a strange night? Absolutely. But I can't complain."

"Careful, sir, you'll launch a thousand conspiracy theories with a comment like that."

"Conspiracy theories? Nah. I'm from Louisiana. This is nothing. This is comfortable."

The rumors unfurl in Ruth's mind: Coach Morris used his connections to tamper with the AC. Or the orders to disable the circuit breaker came from NBA higher-ups, who wanted to even the series. Or maybe the whole thing was orchestrated by a brand of sports drink—the one with which Emory Turner has a contract and Darius Lake does not.

They're trying to smoke us out of here.

How many times has the network replayed the clip?

Conspiracy theories do nothing for Ruth. All too well she knows the outcome of a basketball game cannot be reduced to talent and execution alone. It matters when the ref blows the whistle. It matters when the roar of the crowd recedes and leaves a fan's well-timed insult ringing in a player's ears. And it matters when, deep beneath the court, in the arena's mechanical underworld, smoke begins to rise.

Darius Lake returns in the fourth quarter, agony carved into his face. He hobbles and Ruth's legs ache in sympathy. After a shaky layup Darius lands and stands frozen on one foot while his teammates chase the ball up-court. Ruth is relieved when Bell pulls him out. With seven minutes on the clock, it's a smart decision: better to give up a single game than risk injury and lose the rest.

Seattle's fans are howling, fists in the air and hair glued to their foreheads, the volume of their own sweat convincing them they worked for this. And Ruth gets it, the rising mercury of a fan's emotions. This is among the last games to be played in the old arena; demolition is scheduled for July. This is a team that has dominated the Western Conference for years without winning a championship. When, back in January, Darius played as a Wildcat on Seattle's court for the first time, the jumbotron showed a montage of highlights from his tenure with the Supersonics. A standing ovation was followed by a salute from Darius that almost read as emotional. Emotion-adjacent, for sure. Ruth tells herself no one's cheering for Lake's pain tonight—but damn if it doesn't sound like it! How about a moment of silence? Or some respectful applause as Lake's teammates help him to the bench?

The din pulses in Ruth's ears. The silk of her blouse is plastered to her chest. She doesn't know if she can get through the rest of the night without vomiting; she doesn't know if she will begin her next call to Joel with "I have news!" or "We need to talk;" doesn't know if she needs a doctor's appointment or a tub of prenatal vitamins or an abortion. She knows what she would name a baby boy— she has known for years—but the name is a flicker of a fantasy. Otherwise, her uncertainty is so unconquerable, her panic yields to a sensation of peace. As long as she's here, as long as the clock is running, she's okay.

For the remainder of the game Darius sits expressionless on the bench. He looks down at his fingernails as if longing to gnaw them raw. When he looks up at the scoreboard, scratching at the scruff on his chin, an ice pack slips from his neck and rolls down his back.

The Sonics win in a blowout.

"Your team showed incredible stamina tonight, both mental and physical, as the temperature in the arena rose above ninety degrees. Is there a reason why the Sonics are invulnerable to the weather?"

Spotlights swing around the bowl, illuminating patches of the still-packed stands. Cheers merge with the echoes of cheers; Ruth stands on the toes of her pumps to yell directly into Turner's ear. After processing the question, Emory shakes his head in performed disbelief. "Well, we're a young team. Not me, I'm old, but the rest of the guys are young guns. They're healthy. We come from all over the world—"

Kasey Powell sneaks up behind Emory, a paper cup of water sloshing in his outstretched hand. Ruth, standing at an angle, realizes what's happening a split-second before Powell dumps the water over Turner's head. In a move she can only hope looks clutch on camera, Ruth jumps back to protect her microphone and grabs a towel from the shoulder of a passing rookie. She dabs at Turner's face as she forms her next question.

"You've just been doused by your teammate Kasey Powell, a relatively recent addition to the Sonics lineup. What's it like playing alongside this All-Star?"

Emory lifts his face from the towel. He shakes water from his hair and tells Ruth, "It's no secret I had my issues with the trade. I may have said some things I'm not proud of. In this business, emotions can block common sense. But to come this far, to get another shot at bringing a championship to Seattle . . ."

The Sonics have played in the finals three consecutive years but haven't won a championship since the nineties. How old was Emory in the nineties? Ruth can't bear to do the math.

"I'm not saying Cincinnati's done fighting. They're a good team, but at the end of the day we're better. And when we win, whether it's in five or six or seven games, Kasey will deserve a lot of the credit."

Emory shouts himself hoarse. Ruth bellows back, her voice straining, warbling.

"Speaking of emotions: You've gone on record saying Darius Lake is like a brother to you. A win for Seattle would mean a loss for Darius. Does that ever weigh on you?"

Emory busies himself untucking his jersey from his shorts. The look he finally gives Ruth is admonishing but playful. Meandering photographers stop and encircle them, shutters snapping like rain on a roof. "You have any brothers, RD?"

This is Emory's style: throwing a question back in her face. Ruth admits, "I do."

Her brother, a real estate agent, lives in Indianapolis with his wife and four children. Ruth has opened college accounts for all of them. Her brother has not touched a basketball since high school, but he keeps a copy of Ruth's schedule taped to his fridge and watches every game she works.

"You ever dominate him on the court?"

Ruth fails to repress a smile. It is wide and candid, a complete concession caught on camera. "Thank you, sir, and I'll see you in Cincinnati."

"Thanks, Ruth."

That the entirety of their relationship unfolds on live television is, of course, an illusion: there's no need to wait until Cincinnati. After Ruth has tossed back to Jay in the booth and pulled out her IFB—carefully freeing its translucent, coiled cord from her hair— Emory puts his arm around her shoulders and steers her away from her crew. They form a two-person huddle, instantly attracting a hundred sidelong glances, including Lester's from across the court.

She's expecting Emory to ask if she's okay. Maybe he heard she was feeling sick, or maybe she still looks wan. She plans to blame the heat.

Emory says, "I'm sorry about the other night." His voice is low and conspiratorial. "In the elevator at the hotel? That was not cool."

Ruth feels suddenly light-headed, embarrassed. "No, no. We're totally good."

"But that was you. In the hall."

"Yes," she admits.

"It clicked afterward. Right afterward. I had a lot on my mind, and your hair was different? You didn't have your glasses?"

She lets her head fall briefly, dramatically, against her palm. Her skin is damp, hot like a fever.

"I don't think I have to tell you this is off the record; I know you're not that kind of reporter. But me and Darius were just hanging out. We were playing Fortnite."

Ruth remembers Emory on media day, calling Darius his enemy.

"You don't have to explain," she says. Between them passes an understanding: she won't out him to Roxanne or anyone else. She was never going to. In part because Emory, though fast approaching his professional prime, is still a kid, and Ruth is hardwired to protect anyone younger than herself. She's been that way all her life, from the time she was six years old and compelled to keep an eye on strangers' toddlers, charting their wobbly paths to the top of the slide. And in part because snitching on Emory is not in her best interest, professionally.

"I'm sorry I blew you off," he says. "I was in a mood. Darius and I can't really occupy the same space right now. I thought we could."

Ruth understands. She knows what it means to be officially split from someone while technically in the same room with him— technically doomed to sign autographs by his side in perpetuity. She rests a hand on Emory's arm and backs away, sensing the zoom and focus of a nearby camera lens. She smiles as she disengages, knowing public moments with Emory Turner are always captured, syndicated.

"It'll get easier," she lies.

CHAPTER TEN

If she sees a drugstore she will ask the driver to stop.

They pass a CVS and Ruth says nothing.

If she could, she would consult the Magic 8-Ball she had as a kid, its answers malleable and noncommittal: *Most likely* or *Better not tell you now* or *Ask again later*. The results of the pregnancy test would be unambiguous. Ruth would be forced to make up her mind: do everything within her power to help the embryo thrive in an environment she imagines as parched, rough, crumbling—like a cracked-concrete tennis court, all sagging net and faded lines. Or deny her body's scheming and dreaming: Sorry, pal, we had our chance.

She's exhausted. One night of not knowing won't hurt.

After a few nights in the Juniper, Ruth feels she has always lived among the hotel's whimsically wallpapered walls, its sliding factory doors and low-hanging light fixtures; her own home is a distant memory, dimensions vague and smells unsummonable. As she rides the elevator up to her room she dials Joel. She will leave a message for him to hear first thing in the morning. The message will reveal nothing.

She slides her keycard into the door. The green light flashes. On the other side of the door a phone is ringing, not exactly in tandem with the ringing in her ear but on a slight delay. Ruth pushes into the room and sees him there, sprawled across the still-made bed.

Joel boards airplanes as casually as he calls a cab. His surplus of frequent flyer miles gains him access to as many of Ruth's rare spare hours as he wants. Never knowing when she will open a door and discover him behind it has turned door-opening into an act of erotic suspense. Seeing him now, Ruth wishes she was still oblivious to the projects of her body. She would like to kiss him without guilt, without registering each second as a deliberate omission.

The air in the room is humid and shampoo-sweet. Joel's T-shirt, plain white, is the kind he buys compulsively from drugstores when he travels.

"You," Ruth says with reverence. She drops her backpack on the floor.

Joel looks up at her with a lazy, satisfied smile—cat, canary. "I was going to stay home tonight. And then I thought, why sleep alone when there's a bed in Seattle with Ruth in it?"

Flirtation embarrasses her. She suspects the bone-dry irony of her first marriage zapped her appetite for it. When Joel gets coy, Ruth counters with physical affection. And because the nausea has temporarily faded, or because Ruth is left with the sense that tonight was historical and convinced that historical is approximate to wonderful, she sinks into him easily.

Joel's skin is warm from his shower. Ruth's is cold from the arctic hotel lobby. She presses the length of herself against him, her body somehow missing the heat of the arena.

"I should shower," she says into his neck. "I've been sweating all night. AC was busted."

"Don't shower. Get naked, but don't shower."

"I'm so gross."

"So be gross."

They kiss and unzip. Pulling the waistband of her tights away from her ribcage, she frees her belly, her ass, her thighs from the vise-grip of the hosiery. The release is so climactic Ruth groans and laughs. Joel tugs her back into bed, his fingers tracing the inflamed indentations in her flesh.

At sex, Joel is unpredictable. Some nights he trembles and fumbles and comes too soon. Other times he catches her by surprise with his assertiveness, eliciting gasps that draw Ruth's attention to herself—not unpleasantly—as he pushes and pulls her into position. Ruth likes it both ways. She finds his off-nights endearing, and though the duration of Joel's own pleasure varies, he always takes his time with her. What distracts her, afterward, is the mystery of what has emboldened or unnerved him. She suspects it's her. She should look for patterns, nail down a formula. But she's always so tired, and so ready to forget herself.

Tonight, she can't forget herself. She feels plural. She's multiplying. Maybe it won't last; at her age, almost half of all pregnancies end in miscarriage. And maybe she won't let it last, because at her age she risks birth defects, gestational diabetes, complicated labor. (And twins, fucking twins.) And maybe, in some dark corner of her immutable superstition Ruth suspects the pregnancy is what she must give up to get what she really wants. A baby would be a temptation, a test. A sharp pull on the chain around her neck, forcing Ruth to prove herself.

Joel pushes into her. Condomless, because she waved him off, as she often does. Ruth thinks she remembers reading that the latex in condoms might harm a fetus. And if she's not pregnant, then surely she can't become pregnant; if the puking and aching and fatigue and weight gain have some other source, then surely the source (perimenopause? Lyme disease?) indicates infertility.

The night she first met Joel, Ruth was in a mood. She had spent the day in airports, each flight repeatedly delayed in increments of ten minutes. On the final leg of her trip her neighbor in first class had said, "I recognize your voice. Are you on TV?" When Ruth told him, "I'm a reporter for the NBA," the man blinked, shook his balding head, and said, "No, that's not it." Then a concierge at the Juniper Portland had given Ruth's room to a reality television star of already-fading relevance. Her own fame was still cultish; the concierge had no idea who she was.

It happened that Joel Fernandez was in town for a meeting. Slumped inconspicuously on the lobby's couch between the Foosball table and the vintage photo-booth, he recognized her name. He gave Ruth the keycard to the penthouse and detained her in the lobby, chatting about Portland's ceaseless rain and the particular brand of suitcase Ruth was rolling over the polished concrete floor. Ruth is sure she fixed Joel with the smile she gives to fans approaching her after a game, or to her daughter's boyfriends. The smile is involuntary, often photographed, and always a shock to see on her own face (it belongs to her mother). Beatific and defensive: *I'm thrilled, I swear.*

Finally, Ruth pressed the button for the elevator and Joel passed her a palm-warmed business card. "Let's have dinner sometime. I'm based in San Francisco, but I'm like you, I get around. Text me?"

Ruth could not have charmed him with her deadened airport eyes or her minimal tolerance of small talk, therefore his interest was in Ruth Devon, a woman he knew to be attentive and well-groomed on national television.

"I would," Ruth said, "but I've recently sworn off dating."

Joel cocked his head. He was thirty-three years old and baby-faced. Any law-fearing bartender would card him. Already Ruth could hear the contrived snort with which he would wrestle a scuffed California state driver's license from his wallet.

"Why?" he demanded.

The elevator doors slid open, and Joel extended a skinny arm to hold them in place.

"Well, initially I swore off dating NBA fans. Then I realized I don't know any men who aren't NBA fans. So now it's a moratorium on dating period."

It wasn't that she didn't like to talk about basketball. In a perfect world, she would talk about little else. The problem was that no man of any age (she had experimented within a wide bracket) could discuss basketball with Ruth Devon without endeavoring to catch her in a moment of ignorance. Men quizzed her; they doubted her; they argued with her. Either about something so specific that a quick Google search proved Ruth correct, or on subjects so well-trodden—Michael versus LeBron; the defense of the nineties versus today's pace-and-space offense—that Ruth had heard it all before.

"I hate basketball," Joel said.

Ruth stared at him, certain he had already contradicted himself but too tired to pinpoint when.

"I don't follow sports. For me, watching a game is like, *Here's a guy running. Here's a guy throwing something. Here's an angry coach chewing a large wad of gum.* The whole spectacle, it doesn't do anything for me."

Ruth stepped into the elevator. "Right," she said, laughing and meaning *wrong*.

Still, they maintained eye contact as the doors closed between them. Still, she messaged the man a month later, after flying into San Francisco the night before a regular-season game. She got to her hotel late and unsatisfied. There were nights when the career that sustained her, that breathed meaning into every red-eye and lost suitcase and traffic jam, became unwanted noise jackhammering in her ears. Her attempts to distract herself from industry news—internet browsing, channel surfing—inevitably returned her attention to basketball. Ruth found Joel's business card in an ink-stained pocket of her backpack and remembered his body. Tall, lean, and commanding in the ritzy-twee lobby of his own hotel, the same frame would appear insubstantial on a basketball court. Ruth imagined him leaping toward the rim, falling and flailing like one of those inflatable hype men stationed outside car dealerships. There was something about Joel's story that did not add up. He hated sports, yet he had recognized Ruth's name? She sent him a text beginning *Riddle me this*, and Joel responded instantly.

I confess: my (much younger) brother plays division three ball for a school in the Midwest. He's been obsessed with you for years. In fact, he's the author of a viral tweet you may remember . . .

Joel linked her to the tweet, already a year old: *I wish Ruth Devon was my mom.* Underneath was a reply Ruth had no memory of sending: *Honored, but would never try to replace your mother!* She scrolled through Matthew's timeline until she found a link to his Instagram, where she discovered a trove of Fernandez family photographs, including one of Joel holding a newborn niece in his hands, gazing at the infant with astonishment and hunger.

Ruth asked Joel to meet her for a drink in the hotel bar, which became a drink in her room when the bar turned out to be closed for renovations. Bourbon in her room became sex between crisp, expensive sheets whose whiff of bleach evoked temporality, nonmonogamy. It should have been a one-night stand. The thing was, Ruth couldn't remember the last time she had slept with someone who did not actively salivate over the concept of her rather than the flesh-and-bone of her, who did not explore her body as a cultural artifact, public property, saying something like, "Now I've seen Ruth Devon naked" in the minutes after orgasm. Joel made her feel young and anonymous. He stroked the stretch marks on the side of her breast and said, "I have some of those," pointing to three peach-pink squiggles on his left hip. That night was one she has often thought she would like to relive, moment by moment, exactly as it was.

In another hotel bed, with his fingers where she wants them, she almost does.

Afterward, Joel wants to know why Ruth winced when he covered her breast with his palm. Ruth remembers the current of pain that zipped through her nipple, electric and familiar. "It felt weird for a second," she says. "I've had a lot of random aches and pains tonight. I guess I'm getting old."

Joel considers but dismisses the possibility. "Nope. You're getting tired. You don't sleep."

It's 2:00 a.m.; Ruth can't argue. "Can we sleep in tomorrow? My flight's not until late."

"Yes. I made a brunch reservation for noon."

Ruth doesn't want brunch so much as she wants black coffee and cinnamon donuts in bed. Brunch means mascara. Brunch means a stranger hovering over their table asking Ruth to record his outgoing voicemail greeting. It takes Ruth a second to say "Sounds great," and her hesitation makes room for a longer, heavier silence. The kind that has been swelling between her and Joel every time they try to talk.

The baby can be acknowledged later, when Ruth is someone's pregnant fiancée rather than someone's pregnant girlfriend. Her disappointment over not getting Lester's job—read: her devastation, her enamel-destroying rage—can be dealt with when it happens. For now, she should indulge in the thrill of accepting Joel's proposal. She wants to marry him, as surely as she wants to feel a fetus kick from the inside. Until now, she has kept Joel at a slight distance: There are things she has not asked him, and even more things she has not told him. She has been savoring the pleasure of these things to be uncovered, dug up, confessed; but isn't now the time?

Her nerves are worthy of the foul line: shoulders tensing, stomach knotting itself. By kissing Joel's freckled shoulder, she breaks the tension if not the silence.

"Again," Joel says, imitating his youngest niece, Mira, whom they babysat one weekend in April. "Again" was all the baby said, mostly in response to phenomena Ruth and Joel could not control: birds singing, sirens wailing, baristas steaming milk.

Ruth kisses him again. She takes the detour. "How is that kid?"

"She's good. I spent yesterday morning with her, actually. We went to the park, the science museum, the cupcake shop."

"The baby beat."

"She's talking a lot more. She kept saying *ba-lew* cupcake over and over, which was the one color the bakery didn't have. Ended in tears. She's a master manipulator."

Ruth laughs into her pillow. "Does she make you want to be a daddy?" So light and loose, she almost believes her own performance.

Joel rolls to his side and props himself up on one elbow, the posture of a kid focused on a board game. Ruth's question is one to which Joel always gives a different answer. Still, she's expecting some variation on *absolutely*.

"That's something I've been thinking about, actually."

Ruth sits up, pulling the sheet to her chin. She looks at him and waits. She no longer has access to her own expectations.

"I think I'm happy being an uncle? I think maybe it's enough to be close to my sister's kids, available if they need me. And I've been nervous to tell you this, because I don't want you to think that our age difference is, like, convenient for me. It's not that I'm trying to avoid a conflict with someone else down the line. Wanting to marry you and *not* wanting kids are two separate decisions; I've made them independently, I swear. But I'm hoping they both work for you. Is that . . . is that okay?"

Ruth's heart is racing, the phantom panic that follows the mistake you almost make but don't. "In the restaurant the other night . . ."

"I know. I got caught up in the moment. But you're one-and-done, right? You've always said that."

She could tell him. They could walk to a twenty-four-hour drugstore together and buy a pregnancy test. The fancy kind, sensitive to even the slightest presence of HCG hormone, with the pink plastic cap to place demurely over the part of the stick you peed on. It's 2:00 a.m., but they're awake, the night isn't over. It's unfair to withhold a crucial piece of information from the man who wants to marry her—however, in this moment, Ruth would like to hide the information from herself. Who's to say she doesn't have the flu?

Ruth's phone dings on the nightstand. With palpable relief, Joel grabs it. Phillip has sent Ruth a video of her walkout interview with Emory Turner. Her boss has written *Be more charming, Ruth. I dare you.*

"We don't have to watch this," Ruth says.

Joel reaches over and taps play. Together they watch Ruth toweling off a soaked Emory Turner. The picture shrinks to accommodate a screenshot of Emory's tweet from the morning of Game One. Beneath it, Ruth's reply materializes.

Not once has Joel joined the online chorus accusing Ruth of wielding her sexuality on the job. One tweet in particular is lodged in her memory: *Does Ruth Devon think good journalism is slobbering all over every man in the NBA? Because it's embarrassing to watch.* Ruth recognized the name: a woman who used to play for Georgetown back when Ruth was calling games on the radio. The recognition stung. Though Joel has never resented the men in Ruth's professional sphere, she knows he envies basketball itself, the game's hold on her. And in this particular clip, isn't it clear? Ruth is so far from letting it go.

"How do you do that?" Joel asks.

"Do what?"

"Ask people the questions they're most excited to answer."

The compliment is undeserved. On a normal night Ruth pays razor-sharp attention to the game, noting the details that might stand out most to a coach or a player: the defensive scheme altered midgame, the star's excellent shot selection—only threes and dunks—in the fourth quarter. Tonight, sprinting around the arena, she missed a substantial amount of the action.

Ruth shrugs and rolls out of bed. She pulls Joel toward the shower. He likes the water scalding. The steam releases every odor clinging to Ruth's body: sweat and sex and stale perfume. Ruth remembers her best friend from high school, a varsity swimmer, holding her arm above a pot of boiling pasta water and presenting her wrist for Ruth to sniff. Katie's flesh smelled like chlorine year-round, no matter how often she bathed. Her long blond hair was tinted green. Ruth was jealous; she wanted the game of basketball to seep into her pores, alter her chemistry.

Standing naked in the bright lights of the bathroom, Ruth worries Joel will scrutinize her breasts or her abdomen and know, somehow. Know, at least, that she's physically compromised. But Joel is oblivious, happily brushing his teeth and spitting toothpaste directly down the shower drain, a time-saving ritual.

"I've never seen anyone else do that," she tells him.

"My father did it," Joel says, talking around the toothbrush in his mouth. "And his father before him."

"What a legacy," Ruth says, hair plastered to her neck, skin pink.

"Your parents didn't pass down family hygiene secrets?"

"I guess my mom taught me how to shave."

"Really? I didn't think girls needed lessons. Seems pretty straightforward."

"I was eleven. I wore my swimsuit in the bath so she wouldn't see me naked. Cheryl gave me an orange plastic razor and taught me to shave from ankle to knee, no higher. And when the deed was done she said, 'Now that you've shaved once, you have to shave forever, because when the hair grows back it's not the same. It comes in dark and thick and makes you look like a werewolf.'"

Joel chucks his toothbrush over the shower curtain rod. It lands in the bowl of the sink.

"Swish," she says.

"Hm?"

She takes a breath and says, "Not wanting children is big. Bigger than getting married. At a certain point, it's irreversible."

With suds in his stubble, Joel nods. "I know. But I swear you don't have to worry about me changing my mind."

She engages him in the unwavering eye-contact she normally reserves for players she's interviewing. "You say these are separate decisions: marrying me. Not having kids. Are you sure about that? If my sights were set on a late-in-life pregnancy, if I wanted to try IVF or adoption, would you be open to it?"

Joel shakes his head, confident he's landed on the correct answer to her trick question. "No. That's not what I want. I'm not going to put you through all that."

She doesn't need a correct answer; she needs an honest answer. "No kids," she presses. "Not now, not ever?"

"Look, I couldn't stand being a half-assed father. And I'm not sure I have what it takes to be a *good* father, the way my sister's a *good* mom. I know how hard she works. She hasn't slept in years. Maybe it's selfish, but I like my life the way it is."

Ruth's laughter is feeble, shot through with doom, which she hopes Joel misreads as relief. He seems to, squeezing her shoulders and stooping to catch her eye.

"What else are you worried about? That you won't have time to plan a wedding?"

"No!" Ruth is still laughing. "I wouldn't want a wedding."

"No?"

"I don't need a bunch of photos preserving me at peak hotness. I peaked a long time ago, anyway."

He looks her up and down. Groans. "False."

"And I don't need a big crowd paying attention to me—I get that nightly."

"Fine," Joel says. "San Francisco City Hall. My family and Ariana. Lester, if you want. And you're still wearing a dress, and I'm still hiring a photographer." He shakes shampoo from the diminutive bottle into the palm of his hand, massages it into Ruth's scalp.

That she still hasn't said yes or no does not appear to be weighing on him. "Is that true about shaving your legs? The hair grows back thicker?"

"I have no idea. I've shaved every day since."

He looks skeptical, working the shampoo into the ends of her hair. "Seems excessive."

"Nah," Ruth says. "Makes me fast."

When Ruth was young and first married to Lester, she could not fathom the circumstances that might lead to their divorce. It would have to be something dizzying in its corruption: a dead child, an affair, a bout of psychosis. In the end, the problem was clear-cut and banal: She and Lester became very mad at each other. The only way to stop being mad was to break up.

The last years of Ruth's twenties were the first of Lester's forties. Mostly they worked—Ruth as an analyst for college tournaments and a small package of WNBA games; Lester as the assistant coach of the Washington Wizards, a job he had landed after four years at American University. Mostly they were apart. When they were together—after Ariana was in bed, and after the nightly chores of dish-doing and trash-bagging and bill-paying and laundry-folding had been silently divided between them—they fought.

The fights were never about their lives as such. Each spouse was still pretending to admire and support the commitments the other had made; each was, ostensibly, the other's biggest fan. Rather they fought about the bathroom floor, which was carpeted in human hairs and pairs of underwear and towels that, having long since absorbed the puddle to which they were assigned, lay in a twisted heap at the base of the toilet. Lester wanted to hire a cleaning lady. Ruth was constitutionally incapable of hiring a cleaning lady; these were her floors, her hairs, her puddles. She would clean them up herself someday.

They fought about what they owed Ruth's mother, who drove up from Hampton most weekends to babysit. Ruth wanted to send Cheryl on a Caribbean cruise for the holidays and promise not to contact her until the new year. Lester thought the honest thing would be to write her a check each month. "We can't just make everyone our employee," Ruth told him.

"We can, and should, if we're accepting their labor," Lester said.

A few weeks before Ruth turned twenty-nine, they fought about the precise number of nights the family could tolerate her absence. Ruth's childhood friend Katie was getting married the day after the NCAA Championship. Ruth was in the wedding. Her plan was to fly straight from the final game in Minneapolis to Richmond, then drive to Virginia Beach in the middle of the night. As the assistant coach of a playoffs-bound NBA team, Lester might as well have been deployed overseas for all he saw his wife and daughter. Ruth was not counting on him to manage the roster of babysitters and after-school programs, or even to host his own mother, since Ruth's would be at the wedding. She would make the arrangements herself. All she needed was his blessing, which he withheld.

"It's too long to be away," Lester said, two weeks before the championship. "You've spent most of the year on the road already. Pick one—the tournament or the wedding. Your call."

This conversation took place over their Nokia cell phones as Lester drove to the Wizards' practice facility and Ruth sat in traffic on I-95. Ruth was tearful in a way that undermined her credibility, the knowledge of which made her more tearful. "Les, I am calling the game on the country's highest rated network. And I am Katie's motherfucking maid of honor. I can't pick one."

She wanted him to laugh. He did not laugh. He dropped the subject, hung up the phone. In the days before her flight to Minneapolis, when she asked if he was still mad at her, Lester would fake-smile and say "Nope," meaning *yup*. Meaning indefinitely. Ruth returned from Katie's wedding with a hangover and a spring sunburn streaking her cheeks, and Lester declined to kiss her goodbye before flying to Boston. The Wizards lost to the Celtics in Round One. In four humiliating games, their point guard frequently, demonstratively falling on his ass, gesturing for a foul call that wasn't coming. Ruth's insistence on attending Katie's wedding had no bearing on the Wizards' crumbling defense, but in the unspoken narrative of the Devons' marriage, Ruth's two nights in Virginia Beach had cost Lester something he could not get back.

After their now nightly fights, Ruth would retreat to the master bedroom to read articles or watch a game by herself. Still reeling from the argument, she would have trouble concentrating, distracted by the comebacks she did not deploy, moments of rage imperfectly articulated. And then she would think: What if I didn't care? What if she dismissed Lester as she would a rude motorist, or even a colleague with whom she never saw eye-to-eye? Caring what Lester thought of her—whether his heart alighted or hardened when she walked into a room—was optional. It occurred to Ruth after they separated that people in healthy marriages do not take comfort in emotionally divorcing their husbands. *What if this man meant nothing to me?* ought not to have been such an inspiring thought experiment.

During the off-season the year she turned thirty, the network offered her a permanent spot on the sideline of NBA games.

Accepting the offer felt almost counterproductive—she was an announcer, not a reporter—but it was her invitation to the league. As colleagues warned her, Ruth was unlikely to move straight from the college booth to the NBA booth. The standards were higher, and if she wanted to call NBA games she would have to pay her dues. Fans needed to see her face and connect it to her voice—which should probably be higher? Or else deeper. Realistically, it might take years for a blond and bespectacled girl from Virginia to earn their trust.

The night of the offer, Ruth came home with a plan. After Ariana was in bed—thankfully, the girl still slept with a white noise machine whirring like a 747—she would make Lester a drink and lay out the facts. She would be working fifteen NBA games per year. She would not stop announcing WNBA games or college games, unwilling to lose her chops as an analyst. She would hire a maid to come once a week. She would also talk to her mother about establishing a more formal weekend arrangement, and she would find a full-time nanny to work Monday through Friday. All of this—the hiring, the employing—anguished her. Excepting Ruth's own mother—and excepting temporary guests, privy to pre-gleamed countertops and performed harmony—Ruth did not want anyone in her house who did not live there. She hated to think of an outsider stripping the oily sheets from the water-marked mattresses or pulling a comb through Ariana's damp hair. If freeing herself from her family's needs meant assigning those needs to other women— most likely, other mothers, for whose finite maternal resources Ruth would pay—she would take the grimy bathroom. The shavings coating the mirror, the toothbrushes side-lying on the wet edge of the sink. She would rather lean on friends, relatives. Lester, she knew, would disagree.

Ruth stepped inside the house and smelled garlic browning in olive oil. She rounded the corner into the kitchen. Strewn across the countertop were the ingredients for pasta all'Amatriciana; hunched over the stove was Lester. Their daughter, in a periwinkle *Power Puff Girls* hoodie, sat at the island with a math workbook. Happiness overwhelmed Ruth. An announcement climbed her throat, propelled by incautious joy. For a moment she didn't know what it would be. Was she taking a new job or was she calling it quits? Thirty years old. She could have three more babies if she wanted them. They would clamber up the sides of her hospital bed to meet their newest sibling. Ruth's body would dimple and droop, conceal her strength.

"I'm going to be a sideline reporter! I have to learn how to wear lipstick!"

Shit. She sounded like a child.

Lester turned from the stove, his features already compressed with dread. Ruth's heart broke along its fault lines.

"Congratulations."

Ruth stared at him. Had someone died?

Lester said, "They made me head coach."

Turning the memory over in her mind—as she still does, sometimes, when Lester's hand lands on her shoulder, or when a particularly radical comment of his, midbroadcast, takes her breath away—she has trouble understanding what the problem was, exactly. Certainly not money. Their new roles would catapult them into a kind of wealth that, growing up, had struck Ruth as mythical. They could pay maids and babysitters and the mortgage and the car insurance and still have money left over for lavish vacations. For Ariana to attend whatever college she wanted. Maybe they would see less of one another than other families—but couldn't love compensate for hours? Ariana was smart and funny, stubborn and seven—and in another few years, when Ruth had sufficiently dug her heels into the industry, they could have more babies. One more at least. How far Ruth had come from the moment her left knee and body flew in opposite directions and she, grief-walloped, believed the rest of her life would be defined by the absence of basketball.

In the kitchen, while the garlic burned and Ariana white-knuckled the edges of a barstool, they finally fought about their lives as such. The problem was not money or even time, but rather Ruth. She was supposed to be there when Ariana got home from school, snacks arranged on a cutting board, pen poised to sign permission slips. And also when the washing machine flooded, before the suds ruined everyone's shoes. And definitely when Lester called the house in the middle of the day, unable to remember his own social security number.

Ruth could not argue because she did not disagree. She had wanted to be a housewife. And not in the idle way of girls dreaming up sweet-smelling infants, husbands with bouquets of roses ever-clenched in their fists, but deliberately, with her eyes wide open. Ruth knew she was cut out for the work. The twenty-four-hour shifts. The physical feat of changing a riotous toddler's diaper, or of vacuuming crumbs from the dark crevices of the couch while being straddled like a horse. Popsicles melting into the carpet, handprints on the walls. The boneless tantrums. The fevered nights. Ruth had the stamina and the endurance. She wanted all of it.

This other line of work had snuck up on her. Calling basketball games was exhilarating, the way playing basketball had been exhilarating. And while motherhood often demanded the suspension of intellect—a roaring ocean of patience to wash away Ruth's interiority—sports reporting lit up her brain like nothing else. And at the end of the day, Ruth's status as Ariana's mother would go uncontested. As Mom she was irreplaceable, no matter how vibrant the babysitters or indulgent the grandmas. Ruth knew this because she had been, still was, someone's daughter.

If she walked away from the league, the loss would be permanent. Everyone on the sideline is replaceable—especially the girl.

From his wallet Lester withdrew his frequent-flier card, which, galvanized, indicated he had achieved Premium Platinum Status. "Do you know what this means?" Lester's flannel shirt was untucked, his cap on backward, his head already bald. His white cheeks were flushing a bright, panicky red.

Her husband's hysteria took her by surprise, or she would have laughed. "It means you fly a lot," Ruth said.

"It means I fly twenty thousand miles per year. Actually, I do it twice. Per year." Between his fingers the card shook.

"I have the same card," Ruth reminded him.

"My point exactly. That's my exact point, Ruthie. Only one person per household should have this card. I can't coach an NBA team—I can't be the person I am supposed to be—without knowing that someone is at home prioritizing our family."

Ruth crossed her arms as smoke permeated the air. "Why you? Why do you get to keep the card?"

"Because when we got married, you said you wanted to be a mom. You didn't get surgery on your knee and you didn't play overseas. Because you wanted to be a mom, okay? Maybe you were too young to know precisely what you wanted, and maybe my dumb ass should have seen that. But it doesn't matter anymore. The point is moot. You're her mom, okay? Is that okay with you?"

Ariana was crying. Ruth cried too. Lester put a pot of water on the stove, as if Ruth would soon dry her tears and sit down to dinner with her family.

Ruth dried her tears and sat down to dinner with her family.

Ariana, graciously behaving as if they had not, moments earlier, made her out to be the fulcrum of their marital strife, told a story about a second grader named Sadie who had covertly consumed a family-size bag of Skittles at recess, then vomited beneath her desk during a timed spelling test. After dinner, Ruth and Lester sat on the scummy bathroom floor to lean over the edge of the tub and wash their daughter's sun-licked curls. Lester held his hand protectively above Ari's eyes as Ruth poured water over the girl's head. Suds slipped down the delicate arch of her knobbed spine.

When Ariana was asleep, Ruth made herself a large bowl of popcorn, standing directly in front of the microwave, openly defying Lester's anxiety about household appliances causing cancer. She was about to retreat to the room they still called theirs when Lester appeared in the kitchen doorframe, a basketball tucked beneath one arm.

"One-on-one?"

She recognized his version of a truce and left the popcorn in the microwave. She followed Lester out to the driveway. The lights they had installed above the garage doors were bright like a film set. The hoop was NBA regulation—stanchion, tempered glass. For half an hour, their game stayed friendly.

"Cash," Ruth said.

And Lester, instead of grinning in admiration of Ruth's shot or leaning in for a sweaty kiss, grimaced. A minute later, when Ruth was driving toward the basket, Lester called a foul.

Ruth stopped. She dribbled twice. "An offensive foul? Are you serious?"

"You elbowed me in the ribs."

"Nope."

"Come on, it was classic Ruth."

"What's that supposed to mean?"

"Ruth Landon? Bitch from the District?"

"I barely touched you."

Lester went stiff and silent. The body language was meant to indicate that he (sane) was disengaging from Ruth (crazy). "Fine, fine," he said. "Your ball."

"I think I'm done."

"You're quitting because I called one foul?"

"Who made you the ref?"

"I think my résumé speaks for itself."

She hated him. The hatred had been looming for months, maybe years, a dark cloud encroaching on one corner of the windshield. She had always warded it off, reminding herself that she was flawed, thus culpable. She had, for instance, told Lester that becoming a mother mattered more to her than basketball. She had not meant to imply the two things were mutually exclusive, but maybe, to Lester, they were.

Lester was disappointed in who Ruth had turned out to be. Ruth could relate, and she had always tried to wring that sympathy for traces of love, but she couldn't anymore. A triangle of sweat darkened his gray T-shirt. His bald head gleamed in the lights and his face was rigid with disbelief. She hated this old man who had dared to marry Ruth Landon. She hated his litany of instantly formed opinions—on every blast of a ref's whistle; on whether Ruth's hair looked better up or down; on the best barbecue in Atlanta (and how it compared to the best barbecue in San Antonio); on whether the highest scorer in the WNBA could play garbage-time minutes in the NBA; on which Hollywood blockbuster ought to have won best picture in 1997. She hated the way he rode the highs and lows of their marriage—accepting apologies but not making them, pretending their anger had rolled from their shoulders—without changing any facet of his behavior. Without considering whether he had ever, in his life, been wrong.

He said, "You look like the Kool-Aid man. Maybe you need to rest."

She slammed the ball against the concrete and let it roll into the yard. She flattened her palms against the damp front of his shirt and shoved. He was not surprised, did not fall. Ruth went to try again and he grabbed her wrists and affected a look of paternal exasperation.

"Relax, kid. It's a game."

The man was dead to her.

Maybe it was a game—eight years, a shared mortgage, a little girl with creamy skin and perfect curls—but it was a game Ruth and Lester had lost.

GAME THREE

Cincinnati, Ohio

WILDCATS – SONICS

1-1

CHAPTER ELEVEN

The US Bank Arena, nestled between the interstate and the Ohio River, is not a building of which Ruth retains a mental map; but, as in certain airports, she arrives and finds she knows her way around. She has worked sideline here before, called a game or two. She locates Angie in a dressing room where, after an hour in the chair and an unanswered phone call to her daughter, Ruth hides a backpack containing everything she could need to survive Game Three: Ritz crackers, cinnamon Altoids, a toothbrush, Gatorade, extra makeup—plus various drugs that may or may not alleviate nausea, and which may or may not affect her pregnancy, which she may or may not keep.

And which she still has not confirmed—though, as the days pass, the unpurchased pregnancy test loses its allure, its authority. To pee on a stick seems to Ruth like a gratuitous ritual. A bit of a scam. Doesn't she know her own body?

In the three days since Ruth first became aware of the hormones flooding her system, the nausea has come in waves. Each wave must crest before it breaks, pummeling Ruth on the shore of some bathroom floor. On the flight it was bad. The doggish smell of stale coffee teamed up with a flight attendant's perfume to send Ruth rummaging through her seat pocket for the paper bag stashed behind the menus and optimistic water-landing illustrations. The bathroom in first class was occupied. Ruth shifted in her seat to assess whether anyone was paying attention. Across the aisle, Roxanne was hunched over her laptop, lost in a draft of her Emory-Darius piece. But was the businessman beside her a fan? Were Lester and Jay watching from two rows back? The sickness was a softball spinning in Ruth's stomach, gaining speed, when the door to the toilet folded open and a man emerged wiping his hands on his jacket. Ruth threw herself into the bathroom and slid the lock. Puking in private was a win.

Since landing in Ohio her symptoms have mostly cooperated with Ruth's schedule. Alone in a hotel room, dwelling on the unnerving yet familiar sensation of her uterus being pinched and stretched like pizza dough, any scent, any memory of a scent, might set her off. But throughout yesterday's press conferences, production meetings, and an hour-long appearance on an Ohio network's sports news program, Ruth held the queasiness at bay. The news anchor was an old friend from Georgetown, one of the boys on the basketball team with whom Ruth had gone to the Tombs to drink beer and yell at the television. Laughing with Brian, saying and meaning, "I'm thrilled to be here," Ruth did wonder whether the pregnancy was in her head. A manifestation of her urge to self-sabotage. At this time next year she should be in the booth— not in a milk-sour bed with a newborn at her breast.

Two hours before tip-off, made-up and styled and sucking on a steady succession of mints, Ruth rushes to a theater in the west end of the tunnel. A taped interview with Bell, to be aired before the game and circulated online, was supposed to be Lester's assignment; the two men are assumed to have an unbreakable NBA coaches' bond. But Ruth's director has received a last-minute update from the Wildcats PR staff: Rick Bellantoni wants Ruth instead.

Her stage manager sits them on a behemoth of a couch. The couch is meant for players to slump on, enormous knees splayed as they review past plays. The couch is an odd choice, Ruth thinks. She resents the challenge of sitting with her butt center-cushion, legs crossed, body angled toward Bell but not cold-shouldering the camera. And she resents the optics, which she knows is the point: these people are friends! One of them regrets humiliating the other on live television!

Bell leans into Ruth's space and whispers, "Think they'll make us hug it out?" Ruth's smile is tight. She intends to get over it. For now she stays mad at him. His face—the snowy eyebrows and blotchy, bulbous nose—annoys her. Simone is dressing Ruth with a mic, muttering sarcastically to herself, and Ruth is twisting toward Phillip, Lester, and Jay huddled in one corner. She doesn't want to be a diva but she does want a chair. She would prefer to be filmed from the waist up. On the couch beside her, engrossed in his phone, Rick Bellantoni scratches at one corner of his mouth to dislodge some shard of sauce—barbecue or taco. It's not a smell this time but a sound that does it, the unholy amplification of fingernail against stubble. This isn't happening, Ruth assures herself. *I would never sprint from the room thirty seconds before taping an interview with the most revered coach in the NBA.* But it is, and she does. The first apology is to him: "Bell-I'm-so-sorry-please-excuse-me." The second is to her boss, shouted over her shoulder.

Can she make it to her dressing room? A quick calculation—the upheaval in her belly versus her speed in leather pumps—and yes, she can. Halfway there she senses Lester on her heels, but it's a suspicion she refuses to turn and confirm. Now she's in a stall on her knees. Now she's tying back her hair, the elastic creasing her blond waves. Her muscles contract violently. Her jaw shakes and aches. She wants to sob like a child every time. Wants someone to tuck her into her goddamn bed.

When Ruth exits the stall she finds Lester leaning against a sink, his arms folded and his honey-hued dress shoes pointed gracefully inward. His face is drained of color, of expression. His face is a project in which Ruth is almost compelled to invest, but she ignores the guilt. Let Lester jump to his conclusions. Let Lester be his own problem. For once.

Ruth spins the dial on her combination lock and Lester watches. Ruth brushes her teeth and Lester watches. Ruth touches up her makeup, reteases her hair, dissolves an Altoid on her tongue and Lester watches. Together they walk back to the theater—six minutes have passed, the upper limit of what Phillip might excuse without explanation. Ruth can feel confusion radiating from her ex-husband. He wants to laugh at her, to yell at her, to reach for her hand. She knows him well enough to navigate these trails through the wilderness of his male feelings—but his silence is new. For the first time in Ruth's memory, the man is speechless.

When Ruth reclaims her spot on the couch beside Bell, she's smiling.

As Ruth watches Darius Lake sprint and leap, come off screens and throw crisp chest-passes, calm in the controlled climate of his home arena, her journalistic dispassion yields to joy. Thrumming in her chest, buzzing like neon in her limbs. It's not that she's rooting for the Wildcats. No one at the network gets to root—they willingly signed away those rights. As a kid she was a Celtics fan, recruited by her Boston-born father. It was the era of Larry Bird, and all Ruth wanted was for Bird to win. Even a blowout win, objectively boring, made Ruth's heart swell with pride. Celtics up by thirty? Still a good game. And God, she despaired when they lost! Watching them fold to Philadelphia in Game Seven of the Eastern Conference Finals, preteen Ruth went light-headed with grief. She covered her face with the neck of her sweatshirt, deep-breathed into the bones of her knees. The crowd in the garden broke into a chant: *Beat LA!* Because if the Celtics couldn't win, at least the Sixers could head west and make the Lakers suffer.

Crowds in the eighties sounded the same as they do now. There is no difference in the roar of them, or in the double-stressed syllables of *de-fense*.

Afterward Ruth lay awake seething, reliving each possession, cursing every foul call. In the morning she was exhausted. Her eyes were bloodshot and her jaw ached and her mother wasn't buying it.

"Who is this boy?" Cheryl demanded. "Tell me his name."

"There is no boy," Ruth moaned into her pillow.

Cheryl stood in the glow of the ceramic lamp on Ruth's bedside table, hands to hips as she scrutinized her daughter's heartbreak. "Basketball didn't do this to you."

But it had. It used to. The elation of a win, the ruination of a loss—Ruth doesn't feel it anymore. But she still takes joy in a player at the peak of his powers. In odds defied, score tied, clock running down. Watching highlights she will often locate herself behind the basket, waiting to film her walkout. As the final play unfolds, Ruth Devon's jaw is guaranteed to drop.

Tonight, in the third quarter, her jaw drops in unison with Lester's. They lock eyes across the court, both of them processing the error a half second before the crowd does. Before the offending player himself realizes what has happened.

In the middle of a chaotic play, Emory Turner has collected a loose ball and passed it to his best friend. The pass was not a choice but a reflex, an irrepressible sneeze. Watching him react to the turnover—his hands flying to his head as Darius dunks on a breakaway—is excruciating for Ruth. Basketball is a game of mistakes and corrections, yes, but the fans in Cincy are reveling in the error, chanting "E-MOR-Y" in a taunting melody. It's the moment when Turner, who has seemed rattled all night, proves the wheels have come off.

Ruth is experiencing full-blown synesthesia. The clash of colors on the court—Seattle's lush green versus Cincinnati's high-noon yellow—somehow trigger and affirm and illustrate her nausea. The pandemonium of the bowl merges with the audio in her ear. She shuts her eyes and cups a hand over her right ear to focus on the feedback in her left. Diplomatically, Jay Thomas is saying, "Whether it was an intercepted pass to Powell at the perimeter or Turner actually forgot that Lake's playing for the other team . . . I guess we'll never know."

"Give me a break," Lester says. "Look at Turner's face. The guy is suicidal." Even through Ruth's earpiece she can detect the moment Lester's attitude shifts into fifth gear. Her stomach lurches. "I mean—did the man have a stroke? Passing to a guy who hasn't been on your team since what, November? That's not playoffs basketball. That's sloppy and absurd. Forget about your friend and play ball. Turner should be fined for that nonsense!" Lester's voice climbs a ladder, higher and higher.

Jay, with a nervous chuckle: "That would be a very subjective call, don't you think?"

"Passing to the wrong team? That's not subjective. It's a calamity."

Jay says nothing. Lester, likewise, falls silent, and Ruth knows Phillip has cut in to tell him to take a breather—a reminder Les needs a few times per season but which Ruth, when she takes his place, will never need. She vows it.

It's true that Turner, who is now shooting free throws, appears miserable. He dribbles, tonguing his mouth guard forward and back. His chest rises and falls. He's an emotional player, and Ruth sympathizes. She too played with her finger on the trigger of her own indignation, alert to in-game injustices, any slight or disrespect. It was long after college that Ruth, surveilled by her own success, learned to suppress and conceal the feelings that could be used against her—which, it turned out, included everything but gratitude, humility, and joy.

Behind the basket, high-income Cincy fans try to derail Emory's concentration. They whip towels through the air and wave heart-shaped posters of Emory and Darius in last season's Sonics jerseys, a jagged white line dividing them. They scream *Brick!* and bash their Thundersticks in tandem. And maybe it's working: his limbs look heavy, as if connected to a depleted battery. His shooting motion is stiff. He holds his follow-through as the ball briefly rises then falls a foot short of the rim, plummeting into the paint.

The ref bounces the ball back to Emory.

With a look of disgust, Emory swishes the second.

At the next opportunity Coach Morris calls timeout. As T-shirts are launched into the stands and the Wildcats' wildcat performs dunks off a trampoline, Ruth looks at Lester across the court and shakes her head. A warning. He rolls his eyes in response—she thinks she sees him do it, but maybe she only infers the eye-roll, the same way she can infer the temperature of his breath or the texture of the buzzed nape of his neck. They were married eight years—a run at which Roxanne would wave her hand and say, "You dated. Just say you dated him"—but their marriage never really ended. It's out there, like a hometown or a high school in whose confines Ruth might find herself reimprisoned if she's not careful. The possibility makes her throat tighten, even as she misses him, the same way she misses summer evenings of her youth spent sinking shot after shot, hoping to make a hundred from the free-throw line before the park lights shut off at ten.

Ruth eavesdrops on the home team's huddle, careful to stay out of Morris's line of sight. Several rows above the court a camera shifts in Ruth's direction—she's aware of its gaze bearing down on her but avoids looking into the lens. The army of cameras stationed throughout the bowl, resting on tripods or shoulders or mounted above the backboard, appear in Ruth's dreams as stoic horses, their cylindrical faces looming on the sideline. Stock-still until spooked, then rearing back and swinging their heads from left to right. Ruth steps aside to give this one the view it wants: the unbelievable length of Emory's spine curled over the bench. Massive hands cupping his knees as he grinds his teeth. Seattle is down fourteen. His teammates don't touch him. They hardly look at him.

The action resumes, and though Lester retains baseline levels of sass, calling flops and missed defensive rotations as he sees them, Ruth believes he's in possession of himself. It's a competitive game, with Kasey Powell and Tobin Whitestone compensating for Emory's lapse. Scribbling notes without taking her eyes from the court, Ruth doesn't feel sick; she feels her lungs expanding, the blood in the tips of her ears, the pads of her toes. For the moment, she is blissfully irrelevant on the sideline. At the end of the third quarter she will stop being a spectator in order to interview Bell, asking two questions about Cincy's defense. In his answers the coach will use multiple syllables; he will touch Ruth's shoulder, say her name. Ruth will walk away from the camera believing she has won, that the man will give her no more trouble.

A few minutes into the fourth, Darius steals the ball near half-court, and it's just Emory between him and the rim. Darius leaps, long legs thrashing in the air and connecting with Emory's chin. For the second time tonight Darius dunks emphatically and at Emory's expense, hanging from the rim a beat longer than he needs to. By the time Lake lands, Turner is clutching his jaw in his left hand, circling his right above his head, gesturing for the replay.

"Oh come on," Lester exhales in Ruth's ear. "He wants, what? A flagrant for that?"

"Officials will go to the scorers table and take a look to see whether Lake may have jumped toward Turner with some amount of hostility," Jay says.

"Some amount of hostility? He's six-eight. He jumped to dunk it, caught a body. He can't control who gets in his way."

"A quick look at the film should—"

"I'm so angry I could spit," Lester says. "Turner wants to bring a Finals game to a grinding halt in the fourth quarter so we can watch this moment over and over, dissect it from every angle, argue about it like it's the friggin' Constitution. Why? Because he's upset that his ex-bestie dunked on him? Grow a pair, man."

"Umm," Jay falters, a rare event. "Let's go to the national television big board here and see—"

"Excuse me? You want to go to the big board right now? Let me save you some time: There are games coming up. Between two and four, depending on what happens here tonight. What we have on the floor in front of us is a blatant display of disrespect."

"Who are we disrespecting?" Jay asks. On her monitor Ruth watches the big board dissolve, a move Phillip must have condoned to feign some semblance of unity among the crew.

"The game of basketball," Lester says. "That's who."

There's a pause. Ruth releases a breath, thinking it might be over.

"Let's talk about how we don't do this," Lester says, vigor renewed. Ruth flashes back to their daughter's toddlerhood, to Lester Devon preaching: *We don't stand on the coffee table. We don't shove raisins up our nose. We don't wear our socks as mittens and our mittens as socks.* "We all have things happen in our personal lives. Me, mere moments before this telecast, you would not believe what happened."

Ruth would like to slice her hand across her throat, miming the fatality of a guillotine, but Lester won't look her way, not now, and Ruth knows she will appear in the background of any midcourt shot. All she can do is adjust her posture and fixate on her screen.

"Honest to God, if I told you what happened it would bring you to your knees. But you don't see me derailing an NBA game. You don't see me—"

Jay says, "No, but we certainly *hear* you."

Bell is berating the turned backs of the referees, hopping like a terrier too short to see over the fence. Players loiter near their respective benches, swigging from water bottles and throwing back their heads to watch the dunk replay in perpetuity. Again Darius leaps into the air. Again his legs thrash. Again his New Balances buck ever-closer to Emory's chin. What's clear, from certain angles, is that Emory was poised to protest, preemptively working himself into a rage.

Lester continues: "You think a person is driven. You think they know what they want and that they're going to work hard until they get it. But no. This person—"

Jay: "Just to be clear, we're still talking about six-time All-Star Emory Turner?"

"We're talking about an individual in this building, I'll tell you that much."

"We're going to take a short break for a few words from our sponsors. What's as crispy on the outside as it is moist on the inside? It's the new fish-fillet sandwich from Wendy's." Jay sounds delirious with relief, forever indebted to this fish sandwich.

Ruth hits the talk-back and says to Phillip, "I need a word with Les. Can you open our mics?"

"You want to do the honors, be my guest."

She waits a moment before bringing the mic to her lips. "You're out of your fucking mind."

Lester meets her eyes across the court. From fifty feet Ruth can discern every flare of his nostrils and vibration of his lips, thanks not to the precision of her optometrist but to her intimate knowledge of the man's furrowed face.

"Eh, so I got a bit colorful. I'm a color analyst."

Armed with the knowledge that everything breathed into a mic is a soundbite, that anything recorded can be leaked, Ruth chooses her words with care. "What you're doing? It's not cool."

"Oh, come on. I was speaking in code."

"Code? It doesn't take a mastermind to figure out where your 'personal life' intersects with 'individual in this building.'"

Lester pauses. "I'm feeling a bit shaken up."

"And that's my problem?"

"Yes. You shook me up."

What Ruth can't shake is the feeling that this was inevitable.

That even after their divorce, even on the cusp of retirement, Lester would find a way to hold what she wants just beyond her reach. Only two people per family can carry the gilded card, boast premium status. And what are she and Lester if not a family, beholden still to their stale, moth-gnawed impressions of each other?

"Lester," she says. Meaning *please.*

Ruth knows Jay can hear them. She doesn't care.

"We need to talk," Lester says.

"We'll talk after the game."

"Fine."

Ruth infers the petulance with which he would like to slam the phone into its receiver—were there a phone and were receivers still mounted on walls, perched atop desks. On the floor, the officials make up their minds and call a defensive foul. Emory lets his mouth guard fall from his mouth in disbelief—a gesture so impotent, it's hard to watch. The mouth guard lands near the feet of the closest ref; Emory's lucky he doesn't get ejected. Bell is screaming, "Thank! You! Very! Much!" A dubious use of the last shreds of his vocal cords.

"Lake's dunk will stand and he'll have a chance at a three-point play," Jay says, back on the air.

By the final minutes of the fourth quarter the score is tied, and Ruth feels she has always been a citizen of this basketball game. She was born at tip-off, came of age in the second quarter, wrestled with her demons in the third, and she plans to enjoy these last few minutes of regulation on the edge of her seat. Having lived her whole life in the clamor and clang of the bowl, Ruth has no regrets; other countries seem as fictional as Narnia, as the texts accumulating on her phone. Already Ruth is preparing her question for Emory Turner: "At the end of a game during which you passed to the wrong team, airballed a free throw, hid your face in a towel, amassed five personal fouls and one technical, how did it feel to sink the winning shot?"

But it isn't his shot to take.

Eleven seconds on the clock, and it's Cincinnati's ball.

Cats are down one; the assumption is that Lake will take the inbound, get a screen, and drive toward the rim. Instead, he takes it easy. Casually he dribbles near the logo, waving off the screen and looking his defender Emory Turner dead in the eye. A lump forms in Ruth's throat. She does not root; it doesn't matter to her who wins this game.

Darius steps back fast. Emory hesitates: This can't be the shot Darius wants, a thirty-foot three? Ruth's hand covers her mouth. Emory jumps too late, and Darius gets a good look at a long one, the ball cutting a path so clean that Seattle's defense is already soft and slack-jawed, watching the rotation of the ball, the swish of the net, the scoreboard lighting up siren red.

Ruth will return to this moment in her mind for years: Emory Turner yelling, to no one in particular, "That's lucky! That's lucky!" It's ominous, the way he's both playful and bitter. Something is real and something is staged; but Ruth can no longer say which is which. Then the joy from the bench. Then the cameras raised high in the air, as far as the journalists can stretch, pointed down at the celebratory dog pile.

Ruth heads into the fray to interview Darius Lake before he can wipe the sweat from his forehead or the smirk from his lips.

In Ruth's ear, Lester and Jay spin their own conclusions. "Well," Jay says. "Now that it's all over, would you like to revise your previously stated opinion that tonight was, and I quote, 'not playoffs basketball'?"

A moment of swollen silence before Lester admits, "It was playoffs basketball."

CHAPTER TWELVE

Ruth survives her visit to the Wildcats locker room, where players peel off their jerseys, flinging them over Ruth's head to the mountain of laundry on the floor. She survives both press conferences seated beside Roxanne, whose whispered comments on the players' post-game finery—sweatshirts printed with canceled cartoon characters, flat-billed caps, long necklaces, leather vests, suit jackets paired with shorts—keep Ruth awake. Now she is horizontal on a bench in her dressing room, shoes kicked off, lanyard askew and press pass resting on her shoulder. Behind the skin stretched tight across her temples, her pulse berates her. What she needs is to be airlifted from the arena and dropped upon a hotel bed, like a whale returned to its natural habitat after a decade of Hollywood exploitation. What she gets is Lester Devon not knocking, slamming a basketball against the concrete floor. Ruth's lanyard threatens to strangle her as she rolls to her side to see the Spalding, orange and black and so new it looks sticky, dipped in honey. A perfect object. She wants to touch it.

"I come in peace," Lester says. He has shed his jacket and

loosened his tie. Against her will Ruth pictures him in boxer briefs. When they were married he was the age she is now. At the realization she lets out a noise of displeasure.

"Honest to God, Ruth. I realize I went off script tonight. I realize some of my comments were unprofesh."

Ruth squeezes her eyes shut, so fatigued she feels drunk. "Did you just apologize?"

Lester transfers the basketball from one palm to the other. "I think so. Would you like to play H-O-R-S-E?"

The air between them appears to waver, distorted as if by fumes. "You're fifty-seven. Aren't you tired?"

"No."

"They'll turn the lights off."

"I put in a call. The lights will stay on."

Ruth concentrates on filling and emptying her lungs. She should go buy a pregnancy test. She should call her boyfriend or her daughter, look into acquiring a therapist or a friend who doesn't gossip for a living. But given the option of shooting hoops in an empty arena past midnight, she says yes. Even exhausted, even queasy, even pregnant by mistake, even with her ex-husband, her character permits no other answer. Barefoot, Ruth goes to her locker, lucky number nine. Wanting neither to undress in front of Lester nor endure the awkwardness of asking him to face the wall, she slides into a pair of sneakers—white and coral Air Swoopes, designed for Sheryl in 1997 and recently rereleased—and calls it good.

In the tunnel Lester says, "A new rule I just thought of!" his voice nearly cracking on the lie. Ruth stops. She touches the yellow stripe bisecting the cinder block wall and waits. "I get to ask you a personal question every time you miss a shot."

"What happens when you miss a shot?"

"I get a letter."

"If you're the only one amassing letters, don't I win automatically?"

"Yes. Does that ruin it?"

Ruth drops her hand from the wall. "No. I like winning."

The bowl looks smaller when empty, revealing itself as a space with boundaries and edges. Turns out, the fans do not rise indefinitely heavenward; the roar of them is not a weather pattern. Ruth is aware of her own nerve endings: it's the way she used to feel in church when the congregation fell silent. She throws back her head as she crosses the court, looking toward the rafters where birds fly and nest among the suspended banners and jerseys and American flags, knowing or not knowing that beyond this vaulted sky with its corrosive slants of light exists the real thing.

Lester takes his first shot from the dead center of the free-throw line, hands on the ball, feet on the floor. Eyes wide open: a truce. He swishes it, and Ruth smirks and duplicates it—no one gets an H; no one inquires about the other's reproductive health; no one pleads the fifth or for a dare instead.

Lester's second shot is a corner three. Ruth's spirits deflate; she's too sick for this shit. She tries, and the ball collides with the rim before bouncing out of bounds.

Glancing at the cleaning staff sweeping their way up the stands, Lester lowers his voice and says, "Should I speak in code?"

"Because you're so good at codes," Ruth says, jogging to retrieve the ball. Over the last twenty-four hours, her breasts have become so sore she must repress an instinct to cradle them in one arm. She returns to Lester's side and awaits his question, knowing he will avoid asking it outright, avoid looking her in the eye, avoid admitting that the idea of Ruth pregnant with another man's child makes him want to sink through the court, polished to the sheen of melted butter, and never rise again.

"So you're getting a cat," he says, eyes roaming the sideline.

She presses her palms into the grain of the ball. "Maybe I have the flu."

"I've seen you when you have the flu and I've seen you when you're getting a cat."

"I haven't taken a test yet."

"But you're late?"

Ruth throws the ball at Lester's chest. He catches it. "That's a separate question."

They are standing in the post, almost directly beneath the basket. Lester closes his eyes and, as efficiently as if he were reaching for a book from the top shelf, gets a bucket. But Ruth too has memorized the mechanics of an uncontested shot this close to the rim. With her breasts aching and her stomach sour, she mimics him.

Sticking out his jaw, blowing into his nostrils, Lester snatches the rebound and dribbles, daring Ruth to defend him.

As a kid, the basketball court was the place where Ruth loved herself. Hooping was meditative, and on the best nights she would slip into a reverie, pretending to play all five positions on the floor. (And she was also the coach, tough-loving from the sideline; the fan pumping a fist in the air; the ref putting crucial seconds back on the clock.) With Lester, basketball is something else. When she plays in front of him, it's always the day they met: Ruth the purest version of herself, Lester in awe of his luck. Both of them off-limits to each other.

She plays along as he tries to cross her up, showing off for an imagined audience or his ex-wife alone—who knows? Ruth refuses to fall on her ass but also fails to stay with him as he goes in for a layup.

"Late. Sore. Can't stop puking. Can we go back to playing H-O-R-S-E? I'm tired."

Tired, and mortified to be discussing her aging body with her ex-husband, ex-coach. How she, one or two years shy of the year when it surely would not have mattered, allowed her boyfriend to come inside her. How she ignored the twinges, the surges, the absence of blood until her head was in the toilet. How she will never get what she wants professionally because she has a body that gets knocked up and produces hormones that make her want to stay that way. It's with conception, not labor, that women themselves are reborn. You pee on a stick, watch the second line materialize, and *now* you can start from the beginning. Now you can do one thing right.

Lester tucks the ball beneath his arm and leads her to the padded courtside seats. These are the remortgage-your-house seats, the sit-beside-Beyoncé seats. They are more comfortable than you think. Ruth sits, and Lester looms over her, pacing in anxious circles, a configuration that feels natural to them both.

"Do you want a cat?" Lester asks, eyebrows asymmetrical. Lips gathered to one side.

For a moment, Ruth forgets the code. *A dog, if anything*, she almost says before she tells him the truth. "When you put it like that, like you're offering me a bowl of ice cream, then yes. I do."

Lester's expression does not change, but he looks from side to side as if awaiting a punchline. "You already have one."

"Ha," Ruth says. Because it's been a lifetime since she had a baby fused to her hip—and though she can still feel the muscular ache pulling her body downward and to the right, she has never claimed her daughter's youth went by fast. Most memories feel as distant and dreamlike as anything from Ruth's own childhood.

"I always wanted more," Ruth says.

"Eighteen years after the first?"

"No. I thought I would reach a point, ideally in my thirties, when I didn't have to work so hard. When I could actually afford to take a year off. I thought I would meet some previously unattainable goal and be happy and think: now, motherhood. But goals beget goals, I guess. It feels like there's always *one* more thing I need to be satisfied."

Lester is rocking on his heels, impatient for his turn to speak. Ruth talks faster. "I know there are ways. I know I could work through the pregnancy, take a leave of absence in the new year, come back in time to report on the finals. But I—"

"You want my job," he says.

Lester closes his eyes, savoring the pleasure of stunning her. Maybe it's all each of them has ever wanted—to leave the other speechless.

"I didn't know you knew," she says.

"I guessed."

"I see." Except he never guesses.

"And Phillip told me in Seattle."

"Bastard." And it does sting, the betrayal. Were they laughing at her? Praising her? Wagering on her? Ruth can't imagine a scenario that isn't patronizing.

"You can't ask to take leave your first year in the booth. They'll say congratulations and offer you a photocopy of your old contract. They'll pick someone else to call those games."

Ruth folds in half, stretching her spine as she reaches for the toes of her sneakers. If she stays pregnant, this pose will prove impossible in a few months. Staying pregnant would be the most passive approach to her problem. All she has to do is nothing, and her body will build a human being from scratch.

Lester kneels. When Ruth lifts her head, they are eye-to-eye. "Look," he says. "I don't want to tell you what to do. I've tried that before and it didn't go so well for me."

The janitors have dragged their last trash bags through the nose-bleeds and onto the concourse, letting metal doors clang behind them in erratic succession. Ruth expects darkness to obliterate them before Lester can finish saying what he's saying. But the lights stay on, because Lester put in a call. Ruth will always listen, because he will always have put in a call.

"The network asked me to weigh in," he says.

Ruth looks at him. Hope assures her that Lester Devon gets what he wants—if he wants Ruth in the booth, then into the booth she goes. Despair pulls up the tape of Lester running his mouth on air, free-associating as some kind of self-guided talk therapy. Despair uploads the footage to YouTube and types the caption: LESTER DEVON REVEALS EX-WIFE'S PREGNANCY TO AMERICA.

"What did you tell them?" Ruth asks, bracing herself.

Lester puts a hand on her knee. "I told them it should be you. I told them to give every last one of my games to Ruth Devon. Next year, if it's anyone but you and Jay calling the finals, I swear to God I will change the channel. I will get a Twitter and I'll tell all the other twits to change the channel too. You've worked harder than anyone else. You know more about the players than their own mothers. You're generous and you're open-minded, and, Ruth, it pains me to say this, but I'm saying it: you have forgotten more about the game of basketball than I will ever know."

This is the same man who, upon accepting the seat he is now vacating, told Ruth she was not a good analyst. Too buttoned-up, censored, and cold. Ruth doesn't believe in transformations. Growth, sure. Skills development, absolutely. But within the last week alone, Lester has been both the man on the conference call arguing for Ruth's promotion and the media personality improvising a near-death to her name.

He puts a second hand on her second knee. She appreciates the closeness of him, the physicality of him. She would like to take those hands in hers. Heat would seep from her belly to her pelvis and she would feel that first-love certainty of her body requiring his. She doesn't deny this longing or think much of it; her lust coexists with a disinterest in the inner-workings of Lester's mind. If she's honest, she doesn't want to know, doesn't care, how he feels about her pregnancy.

She can't afford not to care about his influence at the network.

"I appreciate that," Ruth says. "And I don't have any concrete answers for you right now. What I will say is that, if they make me an offer? I can't really imagine turning it down."

Lester rearranges his eyebrows, still wanting something. A sports fan who loathes suspense. "Can I ask you one more question?"

"Sure."

"Does Fernandez want a baby?"

Without pausing for breath, Ruth says, "Joel wants to marry me."

It's not an answer to Lester's question but—for her own sake as much as to torture him—Ruth pretends it is. Too late she realizes the admission is not in her best interest; indulging Lester's belief that her career is something he can snap into a velvet box and present to her with a shit-eating grin is, easily, her best shot at getting the job. She ought to avoid complicating the picture in his mind. She ought to throw herself at the man's customized Adidas as if he were her only hope at happiness.

It is satisfying, though. The way Lester is shocked into honesty, his features in defenseless disarray as he says, "I never pictured you getting married again."

CHAPTER THIRTEEN

In Ariana's most recent Instagram picture, she fixes the camera with a look Ruth is certain no one has ever given a human being with whom they wanted to have sex. It's a look of disdain, or of starvation. A drugged stupor that nonetheless *reads* as sex. When she first sees it, Ruth is in awe of Ariana's coordination. To maintain control over the arch of her eyebrows, the pout of her lips, the angle of her shoulders, the jut of one hip, the contour of an ass check, the flex of her thighs, and the point of her toes—all while frozen in the act of removing the lower half of her bathing suit—must have taken rigorous concentration. But the longer Ruth stares at the picture, the more she hates it. The young woman on the screen is not Ruth's daughter. The young woman is a simulacrum of sex, a product, a fantasy.

A fantasy for whom Ruth is wholly responsible.

She shoves her phone beneath her pillow. If she were still in Seattle, the view from the Juniper would soothe and distract her. But Cincinnati is a ghost town at this hour; even the fast food restaurants have extinguished their extraterrestrial glows. The room itself is generic, the art on the walls abstractly innocuous. Ruth should log into Second Spectrum and watch highlights of the game. She should google "pregnancy vs perimenopause." She should sleep.

It's tempting to imagine her second child as a photo negative of her first: This new kid can't hold still until he has thrown a ball across the yard a hundred times. He sniffles softly when upset, never resorting to physical violence, never smacking himself in the face or biting Ruth hard on the shoulder. Pride creeps into his voice when he informs his friends that his mom is Ruth Devon—yes, *that* Ruth Devon. But the fantasy requires Ruth to negate all of Ariana's traits— therefore her son answers the phone in an unenthused monotone. He keeps his distance from Ruth, preferring to watch the game on the opposite end of the couch. Rarely does he crack a joke. Never does he laugh at himself. Worst of all, he is rude to his grandmother.

The question in the back of Ruth's mind has been "Could I be a good mom?" It's the wrong question. The correct question is "*Am* I a good mom?" and the answer, potentially, is no. Because she has not spoken to her daughter since Game Two. Has hardly thought of her since the air conditioner blowout.

Two seasons ago, Ruth was working the conference-semis at the Staples Center. Sonics versus Clippers, Game Six. Twenty minutes to tip-off and the floor was crowded with bodies and basketballs and cameras trailing their cords. Ruth was in a pantsuit, perched on the edge of the media table and talking to an engineer about his new baby at home, his third son. She was wearing her IFB, await- ing any last-minute instructions from Phillip, and she was mentally rehearsing her opener—an update on a big's strained hamstring resulting in changes to the Clippers' starting lineup. Her pocket buzzed. Ariana's name and selfie flashed on the screen. Ruth didn't have time, technically, but one way she tried to make up for her

long-distance mothering was by always—as long as the clock was
not running—picking up her daughter's calls.

"Hi, sweetie. Game's about to start. Everything okay?"

Ariana's choked sobs took Ruth back to those mornings in
the driveway, taxi cab idling. Ruth ducked her head and let her
surroundings fade. "What's wrong? What happened?"

Two more sobs before Ariana managed to gasp, "Noah. Broke.
Up. With me."

Emory Turner jogged by, chasing an errant ball. At the free-throw
line, Darius caught Ruth's eye and waved. The players were still in
their warm-ups, dark green splashed with pink to raise breast cancer
awareness. The sound system was blasting Anderson .Paak.

Noah was a gangly kid who wore three-hundred-dollar hoodies
but appeared to cut his own hair with a steak knife. He and Ariana
had started going out in January. He'd bought her gifts for each of
their monthiverseries: A stuffed elephant. A necklace. Another stuffed
elephant. On Ariana's nightstand lived an empty bottle of Oran-
gina, which their housekeeper kept trying to throw out and which
Ariana had repeatedly, tearfully fished from the trash for reasons Ruth
supposed she could surmise. In a modern world devoid of matchbooks
and ticket stubs, the remains of a beverage, the glass rim of which the
kid's lips had touched, was a keepsake. She got it. She wasn't clueless.

Ariana's sobs sounded like glass breaking. A canyon of regret
split open in Ruth's chest. Her eyes burned and her own chin
wobbled, and Phillip, lodged inside her other ear, said, "Christ,
they changed the lineup again."

Ruth hit the talk-back button. "You have to be kidding me."
No time to rehearse a new segment, she would have to improvise.
She needed the details, stat.

"Oh, fuck." Because she was still talking into her cell phone.

Ruth had thirty seconds. Basketball had warped her sense of time. Could she apologize and console her brokenhearted daughter in thirty seconds?

She released the button on her mic and said, "Not you, Ari. Not you. I was talking to my boss. I know you really cared about Noah. Your first breakup, it's the hardest one. I remember how that feels—like the best thing that's ever happened to you is gone. Forever. But I promise it won't always hurt this bad. You'll feel better before you know it."

Ariana's silence communicated that Ruth's efforts were inadequate. Often, Ruth's tolerance for her own maternal inadequacy was high. Not tonight. Over the phone Ariana's grief was raw, uncultivated. And she was sixteen. For how much longer would Ruth be the first person Ari thought to call?

Ruth's heart raced as she delivered the promise. "I'm coming home tonight, okay? I'll get a red-eye. I'll be there when you wake up."

Not happening. Career suicide—and yet she was relieved. Knowing she was soon to do right by Ariana would enable Ruth to focus on this game.

"Okay," said Ari. Not with a rush of gratitude, but with a whimper.

Ruth spent the game praying for a closeout—but the Clippers dominated on their home court, necessitating a Game Seven in Seattle the night after next. A game Ruth was contractually bound to work, but for which she would be in Washington DC, having already used her phone to book a midnight flight out of LAX. She would finish her post-game interviews and skip the press conference. She would pull Phillip aside at the first possible moment and tell him something had come up. A family emergency. He would understand, he would have to, because he was a new dad. A human being. And he adored Ruth Devon as much as anyone.

"Absolutely not," Phillip said, chopsticks frozen beneath his chin, noodles dangling. Ruth had found him in the greenroom scarfing down a late dinner. She was still dressed for work but had her backpack slung over one shoulder, an accessory that made her feel like a kid appealing to an authority figure. "It's Game Seven. It's the conference-semis. You out of your mind, RD?"

"My kid needs me," Ruth said, deliberately leaving the details opaque, willing Phillip to imagine an expulsion from school or a cold hospital room. Anything but Noah's simpering suburban smirk.

"I need you. Fans need you. The players need you. Jay and *Lester* need you."

Would Phillip prefer she send Lester home in her stead? Ruth was tempted to ask.

Instead she said, "I can think of a dozen women at this network who would be thrilled to take my place Monday night. A dozen women who have earned that chance. Give the game to Dominique, okay? That's my recommendation. I'm going home tonight. I'll be back for the conference finals. You have my word."

Ruth's plane touched down at Dulles at seven-thirty. By nine she was pushing through her own front door, bracing herself for the full-bodied affection of her mother's golden retriever. She found Cheryl sitting cross-legged on the living room couch, surrounded by pages of the newspaper, reading glasses pushed high on her head. She looked for all the world like she lived there—which, Ruth reminded herself, she did.

"Ariana told me you were coming home, but I didn't believe it."

Ruth steadied herself with a breath, unwilling to snap at her mother and crack open their never-ending argument. No matter what Ruth said, Cheryl would always be right.

"Where is she?" Ruth asked.

"Still sleeping," Cheryl answered.

Upstairs, Ariana's room was a den of sorrow: an abandoned bowl of ice cream melting on the nightstand; the contents of several tissue boxes crumpled and strewn across the floor; curtains drawn tight against the May morning. Ruth climbed into Ari's bed projecting confidence but unsure how close she was allowed to get. How close Ariana would want her. Ruth remembered the minutes after Ari was born, when a nurse had finally relinquished the tightly-swaddled infant and Ruth went to peel the pink hat from her daughter's head to see if she had hair. "Don't do that!" admonished the nurse, reaching out as if to slap Ruth's hand.

Ruth's hackles went up. She pressed Ariana to her chest. "*My* baby," she had said, or perhaps hissed. "Not yours."

"My baby," Ruth whispered.

Ariana rolled to face Ruth. Her face was pale, patchy with inflammation. Ariana looked at her mother, sniffled, and in the endearing/infuriating tone of a toddler pushing boundaries asked, "Can we go to the beach?"

It was a Sunday morning. Ariana had school the next day. Getting in the car and checking into a rented room was the last thing Ruth wanted to do with her stolen time. She said yes. Incapable of saying no, she booked two nights in an Ocean City spa hotel. She imagined jogging on the beach and sweating in the steam room and ordering room service, all while Ariana filled her in on the details of her first, fleeting romance. Had the teenagers fessed up to loving each other? Laughed at inside-jokes? Fought often? Gotten detention for kissing in the hall? Had Ariana lost her virginity to this skinny, *Dead Poet Society*–looking boy? (Please, no.) Ruth hadn't liked Noah, but now that he was out of the picture she was prepared to mourn him. To accept and acknowledge his place in the narrative of Ariana's nascent love life.

The fantasy was optimistic. Turned out, Ariana did not go to the sea to wallow but to forget. With Ruth she was warm and chatty and generous, asking about her mother's weeks on the road, her father's most recent viral misstep (referring on-air to a particular point guard's tendency to flop as "woman-like"), and whether a rookie on the Phoenix Suns was really dating a former contestant on *The Bachelor*. Ruth both enjoyed and did not enjoy these conversations. It was heaven to sit beside her daughter on the hotel bed, tangling her fingers in the ends of Ariana's hair while the TV murmured and the ocean roared and the forgiving lamplight rendered the whole scene prematurely nostalgic, already gone. But she also wanted to open her laptop and compare her latest set of notes to the numbers on Second Spectrum, the recaps in *The Athletic*, the bottomless speculation on Twitter. She wanted to close her eyes and strategize. How mad would Phillip be when she returned to the West Coast? How best could she assuage his anger?

By Monday Ruth had stoked herself into a panic. She had texted Phillip twice to apologize. Twice he had ignored her. Ariana made Ruth promise not to watch the game, and though Ruth secretly resented the request, she knew watching the game would effectively transport her to the arena in Seattle; daughter forgotten, Ruth might as well get back on the plane. Instead, late that night, she followed Ariana to the hotel's indoor pool, where they climbed into a hot tub with an ocean view. Ariana reclined with her neck against the slick turquoise tiles, her eyes hidden behind two circles of cucumber.

"Will you take a picture?" Ari asked through her teeth. She had mastered the model's ventriloquism, even then.

"I left my phone in the room," Ruth said. She was dying to check the score.

"Mine's in my robe."

Fully indentured, Ruth heaved herself from the water and dripped over to the lounge chairs on which they'd abandoned their things. The screen fogged over as Ruth took the picture. And retook the picture. In between takes, Ariana plucked the vegetable from her eyes and, with a damp finger, swiped through the images until she felt Ruth had gotten the angle right. When Ari opened the app, Ruth saw her follower count and gasped. The number had doubled since she'd last checked.

"Jesus. When did that happen?"

Ariana's smile was bashful. "A few weeks ago. This girl reposted some of my content, and it kind of took off."

"This girl?"

"Like an influencer."

Ruth watched as Ariana posted the picture and proceeded to refresh the app repeatedly, her lips twitching toward small smiles as the evidence of her popularity filled the screen. In two years Ariana would sign with her agency, but for now Ruth still considered her daughter's modeling a bad habit, one the demands of college would vanquish.

At the thought of college, Ruth's stomach sank. Ariana should have been in school today. Didn't she have homework? How were her grades? When were parent-teacher conferences? Why was Ruth so bad at this? Women often described motherhood as a full-time job. For Ruth, it wasn't even a hobby.

"Put down the phone for a second," Ruth said.

Ariana placed the phone at a safe distance from the water. She turned to her mother with an exaggerated smile.

"All those people looking at you, commenting on your appearance, does it ever make you feel . . . I don't know, overexposed?" Ruth asked.

Ari shook her head. "No. I get to pick what people see."

"But there are so many of them. And all they're interested in is your face. Your body."

Ariana's eyes drifted toward the ceiling. She sank deeper into the tub, burying her chin in foam. "I know I don't look like that in real life. I'm not, like, delusional."

"Ari, you're beautiful in real life. That's not my point."

"Insta is great, because on there I'm in control of what I look like. And what I say and how people see me. Every new follower is like a point, and if I get enough points, I'll be successful. That's just how things work now."

Ruth was scared that if she said too much, Ariana would stop talking. And she was scared that if she said nothing, Ariana would ruin her life.

"Successful at modeling?"

"Yeah, or anything."

Ruth was confused. Her own passion had led to a level of fame that, without the scaffolding of basketball, would have been a night-mare. Did Ariana look at her mother's life and long for the effect without the cause? The fans without the game? Unease washed over Ruth. The water was too hot, the various perfumes and moistur-izers seeping from her child's pores too fragrant.

Ruth said, "What do you want to be when you grow up, Ari? What would make you happy?"

The knobs of Ariana's shoulders rose briefly from the bubbles. "I want to travel everywhere. And meet all kinds of people. And feel good about myself. And make a lot of money, like you."

Ruth wanted those things for her daughter. She did not, in this moment, want to argue with her daughter. Too often she tried to figure out what she thought of Ariana, or what others must think of her—whether Ariana was turning out good or bad. Wouldn't a better mother try harder to understand how it felt to *be* Ariana? To want what she wanted, to get what she got?

Ruth asked, "Is modeling the only career you can imagine for yourself?"

Curls spilled from the pile atop Ariana's head. Her cheeks were flushed. Her eyes were wide and Lester's. "No. I think I'd be good at it, though."

This was the end of their conversation, and the start of Ruth's knowledge that she would, ultimately, do nothing to undermine her daughter's confidence. For all of Ariana's posing and preening, she was savvy in a way Ruth hadn't been at her age. (In deciding where to go to college, seventeen-year-old Ruth had accepted Georgetown's offer in no small part because she liked the colors of the team's uniforms.) It should not have come as a surprise to Ruth Devon that her own daughter intended to follow her dreams to the end of the earth and back. Ruth only wished that Ari's talents had less to do with the pout of her lips, with her body mass index, with the silky ditches of her hipbones.

Back in their room, while Ariana took a shower, Ruth was reunited with her phone. The Sonics had won Game Seven and would advance to the conference finals against the San Antonio Spurs. Ruth, who had predicted their victory, was nonetheless stunned she hadn't been there. She opened Twitter and scrolled past highlights of Darius and Emory pick-and-rolls. Past alley-oops and corner threes. Past Coach Hollis Waters tugging on his tie as he scolded the ref. Attached to a tweet of a single blushing emoji was a video of Emory's walkout. Ruth hit *play* faster than she could assess whether she really wanted to.

Ruth had told Phillip to give the assignment to Dominique

Lord—a thirty-six-year-old Black reporter whom Ruth had known since Dom was a kid fresh out of J-school. On the sideline of WNBA games, Dominque's combination of warmth and frankness loosened her interviews. She had a unique willingness to meet players where they were, asking "How are you doing tonight?" when there was no other question they wanted to answer. Ruth was sure she would handle the pandemonium of the playoffs with poise and perceptiveness. But Phillip had gone with Brittany Glass, an anchor the network had poached from Fox a year earlier.

Brittany was a fan favorite, but she lacked postseason experience. Flustered under pressure, she asked Emory Turner about a "beautiful outlet pass" to Tobin Whitestone. A competent question—except that Emory's pass had not been to Tobin. Emory had passed the ball to Chris Washington. Both Chris and Tobin had entered the NBA four years ago. They had similar haircuts. Emory balked, offended. "When I passed the ball to *who*, now?" His side-eye would be preserved in a GIF, repurposed for replies to conservative politicians.

Brittany turned the color of canned beets. "When you passed to Tobin? No—Chris! I'm so sorry. It was Chris. Chris Washington."

By the end of the walkout, the flames on Brittany's face had died down. Emory even thanked her (though not, Ruth noticed, by name). In the scheme of things, it was a small fuckup, and one that would have been forgotten if not for the GIF. Still, Ruth found herself entertaining a conspiracy theory: Had Phillip, with his unrestricted access to Brittany's ear, sabotaged the interview to punish Ruth?

The notion was absurd. Each broadcast was Phillip's baby, the network the love of his life.

In Ruth's hand, her phone dinged.

Get back to Seattle, he had written. *And all will be forgiven.*

GAME FOUR

Cincinnati, Ohio

WILDCATS – SUPERSONICS

2-1

CHAPTER FOURTEEN

Ruth and Emory are in folding chairs at the free-throw line. Facing each other, hours to go until tip-off. Emory is tense. His elbows dig into his quads as he leans forward in his chair, rocking like a ship unwillingly docked. He touches his hair, his face, the back of his neck. While Ruth's stage manager confers with a camera operator, a skills coach—young and white and lanky—jogs across the floor and delivers to Emory a paper bag marked with an *S*. Emory nods his thanks.

In the bag is a sandwich. Peanut butter slathered on thick, jelly a ribbon of crimson between two slices of Wonder bread. In four mechanical bites Emory makes the sandwich disappear. As he crushes the bag in his fist, he catches Ruth's eye. Freezes.

"You want one?"

She laughs. "I'm fine. Thank you."

Emory sustains eye contact, staring down the depths of her hunger. Athletes and pregnant women have cravings in common. "Strawberry or grape?" he asks.

Ruth swallows. "Grape."

Emory turns to the skills coach, charms him with a half smile, a flash of teeth. "Can we hook Ruth up with a PB&J? Grape?"

The coach lifts an eyebrow. He would rather stretch a rookie than fetch a snack for a reporter. "No problem," he says, and jogs back toward the tunnel.

Ruth's stage manager tells her it's time. She shakes some feeling into her crossed leg and takes a breath. The red light shines in her periphery.

"Emory Turner. How are you doing? Are you ready to talk about Game Three?"

Emory's expansive smile is an unconvincing mask. "I'm always ready to talk to you, Ruth."

"It was a tough loss. That last possession, under a minute left, you guys were up one and you got a good look. But you missed it. Next thing you know, Darius Lake grabs the rebound. A little bit of isolation play, and he hits it from over thirty feet."

Emory's smile has evaporated. He's looking at her with clinical boredom, as if listening to a receptionist read his phone number back to him.

"That wasn't good basketball," he says. An official diagnosis.

Ruth's silence hovers attentively.

"It was a bad shot. You say there was an iso? There was no iso. He didn't give me a chance to guard him. That was dishonest basketball. Ask anyone—ask Darius in a few years. He'll tell you."

Looming somewhere behind Ruth is the Sonics PR staff. Ruth can sense their eyes closing, faces falling into splayed hands. The network will rush to get this soundbite online, no question. By tip-off, Emory's comments will have expedited his transformation from rival to villain. Cincy fans will boo every time Emory touches the ball—and Ruth knows the satisfaction of rooting against someone! But she also harbors a soft spot for the players who struggle with their off-court conduct. It takes no effort to imagine her younger self scowling into a lens or muttering into a mic, deriding her opponents. Truth is, Ruth sympathizes with a sore loser.

"You say it was a bad shot—" Her tone is thoughtful, therapeutic—"but it was a game winner."

Emory slumps in his chair and pulls the neck of his hoodie over his mouth. His eyes roll toward the rafters in reluctant consideration. He could redeem himself. He could admit fatigue or jealousy and take it all back—but does he want to?

When Ruth remembers Emory and Darius of past seasons, before the trade split them up, she thinks back to a goofy promo video she filmed with them halfway through their eight years as teammates. The interview was largely scripted, structured like a game show. She quizzed them on each other's favorite foods and most irritating habits. She compared their strained memories of the first time they met. The terms *bromance* and *man crush* left Ruth's lips. Then Ruth presented the players with a garbage bin full of household items. Darius and Emory shot baskets with a football, a loofah, an eggplant, a slinky, a saucepan, a plush Sasquatch in a Sonics jersey, a head of cauliflower. The immediate, unselfconscious pleasure they took in the game was obvious, their rotation of trash talk and high fives mesmerizing. So much raucous laughter reminded Ruth of partnering with her best friend for a school project or staying home alone with her brother. She could not resist calling a bank shot with a bag of Basmati rice, and when the bag slid down the glass and tumbled through the net, Ruth threw her arms in the air. Emory roared her name.

What's clear, now, is that the headlines have eclipsed the

friendship. By sneering at his former teammate, Emory is trying to start something. Or to turn something real into something demanded by the market. Because an enemy is less distracting than a friend.

In basketball, anyway.

Ruth can't offer him relief. The brothers-to-enemies narrative is one she helped construct—she doesn't deny this. For Emory there is no way out but through, and there is no way through but to win.

"Luck," he says finally. "Not skill. Luck. Next question."

Ruth has infinite questions at the ready. She could ask him about his morning workout or his ever-evolving relationship with Coach Morris. His new signature shoe. His nearness to breaking the record for triple-doubles in a postseason. The video of him and his two daughters lip-syncing to the *Moana* soundtrack. She could simply ask him how he is. It's tempting to treat him like a buddy—to let her shoulders unfurl and expression soften and say, "Emory, how's it going?" Sometimes, it's the right call. But today, wanting the network's approval more than Emory's, she lingers on the player's frustration. It's not her job to lead Emory out of it, but to bring viewers into it.

"You and Darius, the leaders of your respective teams, are under a tremendous amount of scrutiny. You're expected to be players first, humans second. Is there anything you want to say to the fans who might not understand that kind of pressure?"

The word *pressure* triggers a response Ruth has heard from Emory before. "Pressure? This isn't pressure. I'm the youngest of four boys. Single mom. She cleaned houses. She cleaned houses even when we had the flu. Even when *she* had the flu. Pressure was her putting food on the table. Pressure was making sure I got that offer from Duke."

She wants to tell him that he's allowed to experience this, too, as pressure. Contrary to frequent tweets chastising him for perceived ingratitude—strangers citing his wealth and stardom, his boyish fantasy of a career—he is allowed to feel burdened by those anonymous eyes always watching, waiting.

"So you don't experience public criticism as pressure?"

Silence follows, but the air isn't dead; the air is fraught, taut with possibility.

"It's a distraction. It's noise. One more thing to block out."

"When you're on the court, and it's the finals, and you're playing against your best friend, is it possible to block out the noise?"

Emory's hands grip his knees. He levels Ruth with a look, and now she knows she has him. He's speaking to her alone.

"The NBA is a business, okay? And getting my team to the finals, that's my job. Winning tonight is my job. It doesn't matter who's on the other team. Bell could put my mom in the game and I'd still win. But this is a job I've given my whole life to. My time, my energy. My family's time and their energy. My body and my mental health. So what happens on the court isn't always going to be pretty; it can't always be some cold transaction between emotionless guys—it just can't. We're human. And I'm not apologizing for that."

Over Emory's shoulder Ruth sees the skills coach return, paper bag swinging from his fist. Ruth's longing for the sandwich has ebbed. Still hungry, she's no longer sure she can keep anything down.

"Thank you, Emory," she says.

🎤

Before calling Ariana from the greenroom, Ruth checks the app that tracks the location of her daughter's phone. For years, Ruth would have given anything for a portable crystal ball, the ability to spy on her kid. Both to alleviate her anxiety—Ari was safe, not sobbing—and because she was curious: was Ari kind to other children? Did her teachers favor or resent her? Now, with the combination of the tracking app and Ariana's social media accounts, Ruth's surveillance of her daughter is more tantalizing than satisfying. She can see where Ariana is. Whether she has tweeted or liked other people's tweets or responded to inquiries about her skincare routine. What good is this information, really? Her daughter is alive, chin dipped periodically toward her phone. The confirmation, though comforting, will never be enough.

Tonight, Ariana's icon is stationary, nestled within a Potomac Falls cul-de-sac. Chandler's house.

Ariana picks up the phone cooing "Hiiii," in that way that signals delight to the people by whom she's surrounded and remoteness to the person, the mom, on the line.

"Where are you?" Ruth asks, as if she can't already picture the two teenagers folded into one corner of a leather sectional, tangle of limbs obscured by a soft blanket.

"I'm just at Chandler's. We're studying for our calculus final and then we're going to watch the game."

Wasn't Ariana through with Chandler? Wasn't she ready to move on from predictable parties in carpeted basements? Ruth supposes it's no mystery: what bores also comforts. And what could be more comforting to Ariana than a skinny boy in sweatpants, rising to socked feet to yell at the game?

"You've been hard to track down lately," Ruth says.

"Yeah, sorry. I have finals, and Manny's been bugging me to stay on top of my social. Especially with the Brandy Melville shoot coming up? I'm taking a bunch of meetings in LA, apparently."

Across the room, Phillip is spreading cream cheese on a bagel while gesticulating at a director. In a corner beneath a panel of flat screen televisions, Roxanne is interviewing Supersonic Tobin Whitestone. Ruth has retreated to the greenroom knowing the presence of her colleagues will prevent her from burdening Ariana with news of the embryo, the pre-sibling about whom Ruth promised her daughter she would never have to worry. (How recently did she make this promise? Ari was maybe fourteen or fifteen, looking askance at her mother after Ruth mentioned her own gynecologist appointment.) It's not that she wants to tell Ariana, but that her daughter is a person to whom Ruth sometimes blurts things out, honesty seeping from her like sweat.

"Remember to prioritize your exams. Those will matter more in the long run," Ruth lies.

"Don't stress. I'm handling it. Honestly, Mom, I'm in a really good place right now. I'm not sure I've ever felt so centered. Manny's really confident this Brandy Melville shoot will open doors for me. I just feel like it's all happening, you know?"

With each of her daughter's claims, Ruth's heart beats a little faster. Ariana is reciting Instagram captions into a cell phone. She has demoted Ruth to audience member, a casual fan to be safeguarded from reality. When it's over, when Ariana has run out of affirmations, Ruth says, "That's great, honey."

"Mom," the diamond-hard brightness suddenly gone from her voice, "are you for sure not coming to graduation?"

Before Ruth became a mother, she expected the primary emotions of motherhood to be love and pride and maybe fear, if only because so much love leaves a person vulnerable to the devastating loss of the source. No one warned Ruth the dominant emotion would, in fact, be guilt. As a mother she understands her own flaws as malignant, her own missteps as violence. Her absence is the worst crime of all. The night Ruth called her first-ever game, Ariana woke up screaming, smacking and scratching at the stitches holding her hairline together. Though Lester calmed her down with a bottle and the last few minutes of *Dumbo*, Ariana fought sleep until Ruth returned to rub circles on her back, to sing, "You Can Close Your Eyes," her voice cracked, compromised by the game.

Sometimes Ruth's absence resulted in a loss for Ruth—the first time Ari peed in the plastic Elmo potty, it was with a babysitter cheering her on—but mostly Ariana was the victim. When Ari's second-grade best friend betrayed her, Ruth was in Minneapolis. When Ari got her first glimpse of herself in braces and passed out cold in the orthodontist's chair, Ruth was in Sacramento. When Cheryl had the audacity to inform Ariana that, unfortunately, yes, Ruth was going to hell, not heaven, maybe purgatory if she really cleaned up her act, Ruth was in Oklahoma City. And when Ari bled through a pair of white denim shorts on a date with a fellow eleven-year-old named Sawyer, Ruth was in Miami. Whenever these reports reached her secondhand, Ruth thought her breastbone would snap.

Now Ruth feels a twinge of irritation toward the high school administrators for the scheduling gaffe. If the ceremony coincides with the championship, how many dads will spend the evening pining for their televisions, hoping to make it home in time for tip-off? She's beginning to resent the graduation march as a concept. Masquerading as a gift to moms, isn't it another test? Like the junior high newsletter's plea for chaperones or the daycare's Mother's Day brunch? If Ruth had been free to don a paper crown and eat a Costco cupcake in the middle of a Friday, she wouldn't have required the daycare's services in the first place.

"Nothing's for sure, sweetie. The Wildcats are leading the series two to one. If they win tonight, they only have to win one more, and it'll all be over. But if Seattle gets this win, they'll take the Wildcats to six games, maybe seven. In which case, yes, I will miss your graduation." *And so will your dad.* She doesn't say it, more willing to collude with Lester's lie than pay the price of exposing it.

"Yeah, that's what Chandler said." Ariana giggles at some muffled contribution of Chandler's.

"You didn't believe him?" Ruth asks.

"I just thought you might know something he doesn't."

"No," Ruth says. "They don't tell me the scores of games that haven't happened yet."

Ariana goes quiet, and Ruth knows she's been too harsh. Condescending, Ariana would say. There are nights when Ruth can't stand talking to her daughter on the phone. The conversations veer too quickly toward argument or else empty affection, neither of which feels natural. As a toddler, Ariana was slow to talk, employing only a handful of garbled words by age two. Ruth had fretted that the speech delay was the result of Ariana tumbling from the weight bench and smacking her skull on the garage floor, but had never voiced this fear to anyone, terrified to hear it validated. Maybe to compensate for the lack of verbal communication, Ruth's daughter was especially physical: quick to kiss her parents' faces, to embrace a babysitter, to take even an unfamiliar child by the hand. Ariana's mastery of body language—whomever she touched, she disarmed—persisted long after she learned to speak. And now Ruth craves the contact. She wants to sit beside her daughter, ankles propped and overlapping on the coffee table. She wants to bump against her in the kitchen, an excuse to spread a hand across the small of her back.

"Welll . . ." Ariana drawls, detaching from her mother. "I hope you make it."

Ruth shuts her eyes. Shame bears down on her. Of course she wants to be at Ari's high school graduation. The cap and gown, the beaming teenager, the indisputable proof that her child endured, did not disappear into the shadowy margins of an unsupervised youth.

"Me too," Ruth says. "I wish I was there right now. I'm flying to Seattle tomorrow night. Can I call you from the gate?"

"I'm actually having dinner with Manny tomorrow."

Ruth's heart clunks, thrown into the wrong gear.

"Just the two of you?"

"Yeah."

"Why?" There is no reason for Manny to take her daughter out to dinner. No reason for Ariana to put on a form-fitting dress and those heinous shoes, to revise the bones of her face and sit across from her booker in a dark restaurant.

"To talk about LA."

"Couldn't you talk on the phone? Or over email?"

"Um, I guess. But he wants to have dinner."

Earlier today, in the car on her way to the arena, Ruth checked Ariana's Instagram. *Sneak peek from last weekend's National Mall shoot*, Ariana had written. Champagne bottle emoji. Confetti emoji. Heart-eyes emoji. (Who was she heart-eyeing? The photographer? Her four hundred thousand followers? Herself?) In the picture Ariana is upright, sort of, body contorted into an unnatural S: shoulders thrown back, butt thrust in the same direction, thumbs stuck through the belt loops of her high-waisted stonewashed Levi's. The jeans were cute, Ruth could admit. But the top. Was it lingerie? Like a sneaker it laced down the middle, revealing a runway of pale flesh, the dead center of her daughter's chest.

Ruth wants to tell her it's over. No more modeling. They will break the contract, pay whatever legal fees. Ariana can take a gap year before college. Go live in Montreal and learn French. Build houses for Habitat for Humanity. Live at home and get a pizza delivery job. Live at home and watch the entirety of Netflix. *Anything*, Ruth wants to say, *but this*.

Phillip is approaching, head tilted with a question.

"Okay," Ruth says, squeezing her eyes shut. "Let's talk soon."

She can't tell Ariana it's over. She has forfeited the right to tell Ariana anything.

CHAPTER FIFTEEN

In past seasons, Emory and Darius would catch each other's eye after a spectacular (or spectacularly bungled) play. They would smirk. Or they would avert their gazes and laugh. The effect, highlighted by each broadcast, was to give viewers the sense of having stumbled upon an extremely high-level pickup game. Tonight, with the pair halved and pitted against each other, it's hard to say whether the effect has been eliminated or heightened. When Darius gets too close, Emory winces and squints in derision, as if the marigold hue of Lake's jersey has burned his retinas. Alternatively, he leans in and blows hot air into Darius's ear canal, eliciting the head-shake of an older brother: *Are you for real?* After a play in which Darius is switched onto Emory in the post, absorbing the contact but failing to affect the shot, Emory holds his hand at a child's height from the floor. "Too little," he screams. "Too damn little."

Since he was a kid at Duke, Emory has tapped his left temple twice (or three times) after making a shot, a ritual both superstitious and ostentatious. In Game Three, to the alarm of Sonics fans, he stopped. The pressure of the finals, Ruth knows, can make your body forget its most basic routines.

Finally, the gesture is back. And here is the Emory Turner from the conference finals against Denver—bending the defense with his ball-handling, hard screens, and post-play, running a flawless two-man game with Kasey Powell. Game Four Emory gets wherever he wants on the court, all elbows and knees, all slash and spin; and when he dunks and hangs from the rim, it's like he's daring the league to redesign the logo.

Ruth sits with her elbow on the media table, two fingers pressed against her temple, increasing their pressure in tandem with Emory's taps. She has no idea who will win this series. One of the many ways in which Ruth's professional self departs from her private self: in basketball, not knowing is ideal.

Toward the end of the first quarter, when Ruth's mind has turned toward her coach interview, her phone shivers across the table with a text from Joel. A link presented without comment.

Knowing she should know better, Ruth follows the link. A headline fills the screen.

WILDCATS COACH RICK BELLANTONI TAPPED TO REPLACE LESTER DEVON IN THE ANNOUNCERS' BOOTH NEXT SEASON.

It's the first quarter and the Sonics are up by twelve. Ruth stares at this headline for five full seconds of regulation until the letters blur, overlap, and vanish into the darkened screen.

Could Bell be less suited to the job? He hates the media. He hates jokes cracked at his own expense.

He hates the three-point shot.

Ruth clears her throat, trying to eradicate a noxious, sticky layer of emotion. At parties, martini in hand, Bell is a delight. He leans against a bar or holds court with his chair pushed back from the table, requesting photos of people's babies and offering restaurant recommendations and laughing like Santa Claus. *That's* who the network wants, Ruth realizes: Rick Bellantoni with no skin in the game and a microphone wrapped around his face.

One minute and forty-two seconds left in the quarter, and the Wildcats call time-out.

Lester, in Ruth's ear: "It's not that Lake isn't bringing his all to this game. We're seeing the same Lake we saw in Games One through Three. The difference is Turner. When Turner isn't suffering from a tragic bout of mental illness, it's clear Seattle is the superior team. You think you're watching Cats versus Sonics . . . but what you're really watching is Turner versus himself."

Jay has no time to respond, mandated to pay tribute to the Wendy's fish sandwich again. Ruth looks across the court, through the bodies of dispersing players, over the head of a tattooed, ponytailed fan who will attempt a half-court shot to win a Subaru Forester. Lester is facing Jay, pontificating through the commercial break. In profile his chin is weakened, melting into his neck. Lester's fading beauty bothers Ruth more than her own. She was never in love with her own.

Did he know? When he kneeled before her courtside seat and covered her knees with his hands, did he know Bell was getting the job?

Ruth's job is to eavesdrop on Cincinnati's huddle. To hover as close to Bell as possible without entering his line of sight. To note the way he berates or bolsters his players, his voice strangled and hydraulic, his cheeks flushing newborn pink. Instead, she wakes up her phone and skims the article.

According to a source at the network, executives took a meeting with the head coach of the Cincinnati Wildcats to gauge his interest in replacing color analyst Lester Devon in the booth this upcoming season.

This news will disappoint Ruth Devon fans, who have long anticipated the promotion of their favorite sideline reporter and occasional announcer to full-time analyst.

Would RD be the woker choice? She's a woman, so yes. But for a job that draws on experience in the league and exhaustive knowledge of the game, the network would be hard-pressed to do better than Bell. Plus, the highly respected coach is likely to bring a wizened, grandfatherly perspective to the game, which fans desperately need after enduring the unfiltered bitching and moaning of Devon all these seasons.

Lester Devon, that is.

The half-court hopeful repeatedly bends his knees, struggling to square his shoulders, to keep from rippling with nervous laughter.

With a slip of her finger Ruth could hit the talk-back button and order Phillip to be straight with her. Are they giving the job to Bell? Were they always waiting, fingers and toes crossed, for a man more famous than Ruth to glance at Lester's seat? And what about seven to seventeen years from now, when Bell finally wanders from the court to close out his lifespan on the cultivated green of a Miami golf course? *Then* can she have the job? Or will she be—picture Ruth approaching sixty, the skin around her eyes like ruined tissue paper—too old?

It frightens her, how close she is to saying these words. She feels drunk or adrift; there would be no consequences because soon there will be no Ruth Devon. If Bell gets the job, she's done. There are other things she can do with her life.

She's panicking, she realizes, moving two fingers from her

temple to her tightening throat. The panic recedes as she acknowledges it; but the longing remains. She wants something she no longer believes she will get.

On the court, the fan bends his knees one last time. His form is good. After so many hesitant dribbles and misleadingly sheepish grins, he shoots. Ruth's eyes follow the ball as it smacks against the backboard and sinks through the net. The man folds in half. Laughing, he unfurls to run a spasmodic victory lap, his brightly inked arms in the air. The stadium announcer could be a wolf howling at the moon.

Across the court from his ex-wife, Lester Devon rises, applauding, unabashed and unequivocally thrilled for this anonymous fan and his brand-new Subaru.

*

At halftime, Cincinnati's general manager—indebted to Ruth since she agreed to let his nineteen-year-old daughter shadow her during a regular season game—ushers her into the locker room. It's a space that evokes Ruth's bedroom in high school, had it been surrounded in mirrors, duplicated ad infinitum. Sneakers avalanche from cabinets too full to close. Damp towels fester on the floor. Draped over tabletops are tangles of cell phone chargers, hoodies, and headphones. Feeling like an intruder amid sacred squalor, Ruth crowds into a corner with the equipment assistants and the high-energy towel boys. She watches Darius Lake cross the room in two steps and sink into his leather swivel chair. Behind him, his locker is conspicuously tidy: street clothes and spare uniforms hung side-by-side, shoes aligned.

One of the few players who still refrains from covertly checking his phone at halftime, Darius is serene as a trainer crouches at his side and wraps an ice pack around his left knee. His teammates sulk toward the toilets or stand before their lockers silently hydrating, excess water slipping down their necks.

Bell enters, flanked by assistant coaches. His is the body language of a mom spontaneously tossing treasured toys into a Hefty bag. He has no clipboard. There will be no calm dissection of pick-and-rolls or turnovers. Although she's not the one in trouble, Ruth braces herself for the bullfrog bellow of his voice.

"How? Many? Minutes? Are in? An NBA game?"

Bell repeats himself, adjusting neither his volume nor his erratic accentuation.

In his vibrational drawl, somewhere between smart-ass and teacher's pet, Darius supplies the answer. "Forty-eight minutes."

Bell echoes his star. "Forty-eight minutes." He grips the edge of a table strewn with empty Gatorade bottles. "So why, twenty-four minutes into a forty-eight minute game, are we lagging? Has every? Last? One of you? Contracted an autoimmune disorder?"

Ruth is often around men who are yelling. She has the ghost of an impulse to reprimand him: be nice, be humane! But who is she to silence Bell? If she had the privilege of assuming her own rage would draw a rapt, contrite audience, wouldn't she exercise it? Easily she can imagine the satisfaction of her emotions ricocheting around the room. And it's hard to argue with the results. Contained within the coach's anger is the truth: the Cats need to get their shit together.

Players squirm, shoulders rising and falling, toes digging ditches into the carpet woven with the Wildcats logo. No mention of Emory Turner torching them. No mention of Seattle's talent running deeper, of one team necessarily being second best. Darius scratches his chin, looks thoughtfully at his left knee encased in a bulbous wad of plastic.

Ruth senses moisture slipping from her body, seeping into the cotton of her underwear. She flinches. Blood.

"I'm not going to remind you how to play basketball," Bell says. "I'm not a miracle worker. You have time to win this game, so do that. Fucking do that, okay? You have time."

The coach shakes as he stomps into his office. Ruth's fingers, wrapped around a ballpoint pen, also shake. She wants to say no. No to her insides contracting. No to pulling down her underwear in the bathroom and seeing the red inkblots of a miscarriage. The force of her aversion to this moment—which she can see so clearly, as if it's already happened—takes her breath away.

She exits the locker room and stands in the hall, awaiting more moisture or the first flares of pain. Officials and interns and journalists move past her, staring straight ahead. Her discomfort makes her anonymous, somehow. The dampness could be discharge. Is vaginal discharge normal in early pregnancy? Is there such thing as normal when you're pregnant at forty-two?

Wildcats flood the hall, moving toward the court with the long-limbed confidence of men who have not recently been cursed out by their coach. As Darius passes, knee de-mummified, Ruth watches his gait. Not a limp or a hobble; still, stiffer than he should be. Ruth feels a dread at the imperfection of the human body— even a near-perfect one.

She follows the team. Emerging from the tunnel into the chaos of the bowl, she feels like a fish caught and released. She returns to the media table, taking inventory of her mic, her notebooks, her pens. She returns to her view of the lights reflected in Lester's bald head. She crosses her legs tightly, as if she can delay her body's decision. Maybe she can.

The way these third-quarter Wildcats hit the floor, you would think halftime had been a crash course in defensive strategy. That Bell had sat them down, drawn X's and O's, talked them through the mechanics of swarming Turner on the block, forcing him to pass or else take jump shots beyond his comfort zone. There is exactly one way to beat the Sonics—Ruth can almost hear Bell say, though he did not say—and it's by keeping Emory Turner away from the rim.

Lester: "There's plenty of time for the momentum of this game to shift." Ruth snorts. Wasn't he the one who declared the Wildcats helpless against an unimpaired Turner?

Through her IFB she can hear a smile underlying Jay's words: "Ladies and gentlemen, Lester Devon, a man who never says anything he can't take back."

What Ruth needs is someone to curse her out. To corner her in a locker room and demand that she wake the fuck up. She's running out of time, letting her body distract her from the likelihood of the network hiring Bell or another ex-coach—someone who has stalked the sideline, suit jacket flapping, spit flying, for decades. Lester may have vouched for her, Phillip may be pulling for her, but the company is vast, full of suits and bald heads and stubborn assumptions.

Those assumptions: Sports belong to men. Women may enjoy sports, but they do so superficially, the way they enjoy *Keeping Up with the Kardashians* and romance novels and watching birds flock to a feeder. When a woman makes her living in proximity to a sport—or plays a sport or watches a game with her fists balled tight—her investment is not necessarily unwelcome. It's just unnatural: a passion she contrived to get closer to manliness, or to redeem an oversized and otherwise monstrous body. Whereas men are born with athletic instincts—competition and domination and saving the day. When Lester Devon tells you a player added a euro step over the summer, Lester understands both the mechanical *how* and the spiritual *why*: the ember-hot motivation fueling the fancy footwork, a player's absolute refusal to lose.

Don't sweat it, ladies. Women know about other shit. They know how it feels to swell and rupture. They know how to love other people more than themselves—something men have only faked, to varying degrees of verisimilitude.

When Ruth thinks about what she wants, what she's asking for, she could laugh. That the network hasn't rushed to hand her a copy of Lester's contract with his name crossed out and hers written in is laughable. Already she works harder than Lester. As an analyst she would double down. Because as an analyst, finally, Ruth will have an outlet for her gluttonous body of NBA knowledge. No more fifteen-second segments or hurried huddle updates: she will weave all she knows into a game-long dialogue, loose and luxurious and, until now, unheard.

She will wake up to emails from PR directors and the network's research department. She will inhale stats, highlight videos, quotes from coaches. When Lester would close his laptop for the morning, Ruth will press on, reading every profile published in the preceding twenty-four hours, committing to memory the idiosyncrasies of each player's game, the meals they carry onto the plane, the news from their hometowns. And in the car on the way to the arena Ruth will catch up on a Memphis point guard's self-produced cooking show, on which he invites his teammates to sample off-putting foods—bull's penis pizza, live cricket tea. She'll watch a Maverick's Instagram stories: the songs lip-synced from the driver's seat of a vintage Impala, the Taco Tuesdays with his kids. If a Cav and his girlfriend call it quits, if a Pelican's baby is born, if a Blazer seeks treatment for his anxiety, Ruth knows. She stalks all of them with extracurricular pride and concern. Not to interrogate them about their personal lives, but to see them and know them. And when she's talking to these men in the strobe-lit aftermath of a win or the swampy heat of a locker room, it's clear to them that she gives a shit. That her curiosity extends beyond the numbers on the board. Players notice. And it's the players who made Ruth who she is, her fame related to the way they look at her on national television, respect evident in their angled jaws.

When journalists write about Ruth, they seem to consult a thesaurus for synonyms of *badass*. In print Ruth has been called confident, gutsy, and intrepid. She's a tough cookie, a tomboy, unflinching and formidable. In Ruth's mind, these words describe not her, exactly, but the kind of woman people assume she must be in order to do what she does. If there's some truth to the characterizations—which, with the exception of one Reddit thread, stop short of accusing Ruth of harboring above-average levels of testosterone—it's that Ruth is competitive. Fiercely, blindingly so. If she could win the job by playing Rick Bellantoni one-on-one, she would wipe the floor with the old man. But to the question *Why you?* Ruth's answer is that she's open. She goes into game days armed with every piece of information available to her, predictions penciled faintly in her mind, but without expectations. Watching the action, Ruth sees not what's supposed to happen but what is happening—whether it's a star underperforming, a rookie combusting, a veteran reliving his glory days, or a reliable sixth man playing through a covert injury. She approaches her interviews with the same openness, prepared to be shut out or let in, confined by a player's ego or loosened by a joke. Ruth is good at her job because she has mastered the art of the split-second reaction. She has no

problem relinquishing control. That Ruth is a woman who understands basketball should not be remarkable; basketball is a sport
that women understand.

Ruth is asking the network for a job she can't help doing. To be
promoted to the role of superfan, which she has compulsively filled
all her life. And yet, if she does nothing, she will be snubbed. The
network will give the gig to a septuagenarian whose voice sounds
ineffably *correct* coughing along with the action. Who could fault
them for it? Say what you will about Rick Bellantoni: the man is
good on television. As Cincy digs out of a thirteen-point hole,
Bell paces in front of his bench, flailing and shouting, towing a
thin line between rage and joy. Ruth can already hear his voice
replacing Lester's in her earpiece, spouting controversial opinions
about All-Stars and female referees, uniting the command of the
hall-of-fame coach with the crankery of your drunk uncle. When
the camera pans to courtside celebrities, Bell will feign ignorance.
What kind of name is Rihanna?

Ruth doesn't have to be there for it. Sticking around is optional.

She imagines calling Phillip and telling him she's pregnant,
taking leave. She can hear the lightness in her producer's voice as
he congratulates her, his relief standing in for the relief of the entire
network. They will pat themselves on the back, assuring one another
they knew she was hiding something—that the circles under her
eyes had darkened for a reason. Bell in the booth, and Ruth pregnant! Who saw that coming? Everyone wins.

If she discovers blood at the end of the night, does she grieve?
Heave a sigh? Find it within herself to try again? Ruth has no
plan. No idea what she wants. A wave of nausea crests as Seattle's
offense falters. Emory misses a shot, and Darius pounces on the
long rebound, batting the ball away from Kasey Powell and flying

up the court for the kind of uncontested dunk featured on posters and video game covers. Still all business, his face impassive and steady. "When Darius Lake retires he should do the voice for meditation apps," says Lester in Ruth's ear, in sports bars and apartment living rooms. "People would pay for the privilege of listening to him feel nothing." Nobody knows, but Lester Devon is an alto, sings with a Sinatra-smoothness that embarrasses his daughter and haunts his ex-wife. Sometimes she expects Lester to split in two. To keep it professional on air while, on her IFB, breaking into song.

The score is tied. There are three minutes left in the third and Seattle calls a timeout. Ruth lingers on the wings of the huddle but learns little. The coaches, mic'ed, are likely revealing more to the production truck than to Ruth, who can't hear much over the agitated roar of the fans, the Lizzo single blasting through the public-address system. She spends the commercial break shifting her weight from one hip to the other, trying to ascertain if she's still bleeding. Was she ever? Is she making things up? Losing her mind would be worse than miscarrying.

From the moment Ruth reclaims her seat, it's clear the timeout mattered. First comes Emory Turner's up-and-under layup, which he punctuates with a stare down directed at his best friend / worst enemy Darius Lake. Teammate Kasey Powell has Turner's back with a clean three. "And just like that," Lester says, "Seattle reminds Cincinnati who they're dealing with."

What Ruth wants, truly, is to put her hands on the child she already has. She wants to see her daughter's face. If she were to book a first-class ticket for Ari to meet her in Seattle in three days— she has the miles—Cheryl would remind Ruth it's not Ariana's job to travel. To swoop in and save the day and make Ruth feel better about her choices. Mothers swoop. Mothers save. And to her credit, Cheryl has done nothing less for Ruth. After her divorce, Ruth called her mother with a not-so-selfless proposal, and Cheryl agreed to move into the house Lester had willingly left to Ruth, to retire years earlier than planned, accepting her daughter's financial support in exchange for on-demand, near-constant childcare.

Cheryl has done everything for Ruth. That Ruth has done everything for her own daughter is an argument no one could make. Apologies have been tumbling from her tongue since the beginning: that first night in the maternity ward, the baby wouldn't stop crying and Ruth said, with calm sincerity, "I'm so sorry."

"For what?" Lester asked, shoulders slumped in that Hawaiian shirt Ruth hated.

"For evicting her," Ruth said.

Emory intercepts a pass and starts the break. An outlet to Kasey for the two-on-one, with Darius backpedaling on defense. "And it's back to Turner at the rim!" Jay screeches in Ruth's ear. "He throws it down!" It's a sublime give-and-go alley-oop; neither player's feet touch the ground while the ball is in his hands. Emory shushes the restive crowd with a finger cocked against his lips.

Ruth's birdcaged heart can barely take it.

CHAPTER SIXTEEN

@HeyRD was practically catatonic in that interview with Bell. Lady might as well wear a Sonics jersey to game five.

Is it just me—or has her professionalism deteriorated RAPIDLY over the series?

Honestly, Ruth Devon looks tired. Maybe she should make like her ex-husband and put down the mic for good?

K, now I'm hearing that she's been harassing network execs for a full-time announcer's contract. Umm . . . how about not?

I don't have a problem with a woman in the booth, I just find her voice SO annoying. And let's be honest—she's never been impartial.

> Agreed! Always obvious who she's rooting for. The way she cozies up to Emory Turner . . . she wants the D. And I don't mean defense.

At the start of the fourth, the game is still tied and Ruth is nervous. She hasn't puked since Game Three but she has come close, bile burning at the back of her throat. Now her mouth is a sea of hot saliva, her eyes watering preemptively. Weighing these symptoms against the blood she's sure she felt between her legs is confusing, infuriating. *Fuck this*, she thinks—*this* being the mystery of her middle-aged body.

Both teams have eighty-nine points. Two minutes pass and the score doesn't change. The Wildcats and Sonics have figured each other out. Both teams have taken away threes and layups; what remains are contested midrange jumpers, fouls at the rim, lots of yapping at the refs. The smell is back. Only the knowledge of the camera panning the floor, catching her in the background of any midcourt shot, prevents Ruth from burying her nose in the sleeve of her dress. She turns when she feels a hand on her shoulder. Seamlessly she breaks out a smile for Patricia O'Connor, radio announcer for the New York Yankees.

"Just saw that article," Patricia says, her Boston accent turning Bronx in disgust. "Hated it."

Ruth throws up her hands. "Just a rumor, right?"

Patricia is clutching a red-and-white-striped sleeve of popcorn. Ruth is interested until she catches a whiff and wants nothing to do with the stuff. Horrible. Patricia squeezes Ruth's shoulder and mouths something profane before moving toward the aisle. Ruth doesn't envy Patricia's ascent to the press box. Twenty or thirty rows above the court, she's always shocked at how quickly the game recedes, the action flattened by distance, secondary to hotdogs and selfies and beer sloshing over the rims of plastic cups. Those high-altitude fans have no access to Jay's play-by-play or Lester's analysis or Ruth's updates; the unhinged caterwauling of the stadium announcer is their sole insight into the action. Ruth thinks she'd rather watch at home, hanging on every word of the broadcast, counting on the ever-shifting camera angles.

In her ear, Jay is enthused over "a skip pass from Kasey Powell," and Ruth whips around in time to see Emory Turner catch the ball at the three-point line and drive hard. He flies toward the rim but two Wildcats are already there, and Emory takes off early, hoping to clear them. His legs meet their shoulders, throwing him off balance.

There's a snap, like wood splitting.

"That looks like—that's a hard fall," Lester stammers. "A hard fall—oh!"

The "oh!" is hopeful. Lester gives himself room to acknowledge an overreaction. He waits for Turner to bounce back. Turner doesn't. Because when he landed his leg buckled beneath him, and now there's a hinge halfway between his knee and his ankle.

"Turner broke his leg," Lester says in one breath. "Turner has broken his leg." Three sharp blasts of the ref's whistle. "Turner has broken his leg."

The camera confirms: flash of flesh, flash of bone. Ruth has stopped breathing. Turner, crumpled like a car totaled on the interstate, slams his back against the court to escape the wreckage of his limb. The monitors show his face constricted in agony: eyes screwed shut, mouth knotted. Did the man scream? Ruth doesn't think so.

In the confusion, Sonics rookie Aaron Thomas has grabbed the rebound and tipped it in—now he sees Emory and his first instinct is to run in the opposite direction, as if a bomb was detonated and the shards are still flying.

After a moment of shocked inactivity, coaches and team doctors rush to Emory's side. Pressure mounts behind Ruth's eyes as she grips the edge of the media table, physically preventing herself from going to him. Tears form and wobble, distorting her vision but not falling. *You barely know him*, she tells herself. *He's not yours.* The crowd's silence yields to a low murmur— twenty thousand subdued laments. Rising above the regret comes scattered applause. Drunken cheers. A riptide of enthusiasm for Emory Turner's fate. Ruth slides out from behind the table, jumps the two steps to the court, and faces the fans. Her expression may be discernible only to those in the first few rows, but with the stretch of her arms and the force of her palms, with an intolerant shake of her head, the cheers die down. The applause becomes erratic, then stops.

Darius has gone to Emory's side. Ruth can't see his face until the monitors fill with it. The man they call stoic, as if it's his epithet, is sobbing. As Seattle's doctors set Emory's leg in an Aircast, players on both teams embrace and kneel and pray. Could have been any one of them, but it was Emory. Could have been any game, but it was Game Four of the NBA finals. The broadcast replays the fall in excruciatingly slow motion. In case you missed it, or in case you need a second look. The choice is Phillip's, and Ruth can't decide if she holds it against him. These men's bodies are the entertainment. These bodies are insured for millions.

These bodies break on national television.

After the replay, the broadcast cuts to the bird's-eye view from the top of the backboard, where the camera has been manipulated to show Emory supine and sprawled in the corner of the paint. Doctors and coaches and Darius surround him, fanned out like petals.

Ruth makes her way across the court, dodging security and stepping over wads of blood-stained towels. In her ear, Phillip cuts through Jay and Lester's somber commentary. "RD, where you headed?"

She doesn't answer. On the outer circle of the group tending to Emory, Ruth stoops and picks up the size-fifteen sky-blue Nike that a doctor pried from Emory's foot and discarded. She watches between pairs of broad male shoulders as the medics lift Emory onto the gurney. Emory doesn't lie back but sits upright, gripping the edges of the bed. The hard set of his jaw is incongruous with his eyes, now wide and disbelieving. The crowd issues a slow, respectful clap as Emory is wheeled toward the tunnel.

As he passes, Ruth touches the player's unbroken leg, his left. Emory looks at her with dim acknowledgment, evoking their encounter in the elevator after Game One, the discrepancy between Ruth's delighted "Hi!" and his own indifference. A few hours ago he secured her a peanut butter sandwich in a brown paper bag. In that moment, he was an All-Star prepping for Game Four, and she was his favorite reporter. Now he is a man whose life has changed, and she is nothing more than a bystander. Ruth is sorry this has happened; she is so sorry, she feels sick.

An equipment assistant approaches. "I'll take that," he says, reaching for the shoe. Ruth gives it up willingly.

Lester is naming the bench player who will check in to replace Emory. "With Ruth Devon reporting, we'll get an update on Emory Turner's status as soon as we can."

Only then does Ruth remember to follow the gurney into the tunnel.

Alison Lee, sideline reporter for Seattle's regional network, is chronically cheerful, her personality carbonated. Even now, each of her sentences ends with an exclamation point: "I'm just realizing that the snapping sound was the bone! I thought it was a glitch in the sound system—like, I thought it was coming through the speakers! That's how loud it was! Did you hear it, Ruth?"

Outside the X-ray room, Supersonics staff push past them and through the door, avoiding their hunger. Ruth nods at Alison. Her expression is vacant as Roxanne compulsively compares Emory's fall to past injuries suffered by other players: Solomon Gay's off-season fracture sustained during a Team USA scrimmage; a Timberwolf's bad luck in the regular season; a college kid's Sweet Sixteen emergency. Solomon returned to the court after nine months. The Minnesota player is still in therapy. The college kid was never heard from again.

Without Emory, the Sonics will lose tonight. They will lose the series. It's a fact supported by statistics and history and by the grief coiled between Ruth's ribs.

If she could, she would tell Emory what a nurse told a twenty-two-year-old Ruth Landon who could not stop sobbing into her hospital pillow: *It's not your fault. Our bodies fail us—even hotshots like you.* Ruth had been unable to look at the nurse, but the words dove deep into her memory, resurfacing as needed. A version of this truth is what Ruth told her own mother the night Cheryl—typically stalwart, secretive—finally consented to one of

Ruth's interviews about the past. On summer evenings, provoked by loneliness and the long off-season, Ruth has a habit of plying her mother with chardonnay and unwanted questions. Last year, she asked her mom about the dead baby whom Cheryl delivered when Ruth and her brother were two and four, respectively. "It must have been hell," Ruth said, twirling the stem of her glass between her fingers.

"It wasn't pleasant," Cheryl admitted.

"It was a tragedy, Mom. A stillbirth. You lost a kid—and you can't admit it broke your heart?"

Cheryl twisted her lips. "Of course it was a tragedy. Of course it broke my heart. But I didn't expect everything to be easy, and so most things weren't that hard. And when they were hard, it's not as if I had all the time in the world to feel sorry for myself. There were no babysitters, no maids on payroll. I went back to work, and I took care of the children I already had, and I moved on. That's something people used to do: move on."

Ruth leaned toward her mother. They were on the patio, the only light coming from the kitchen, filtered through the screen door. "You know it wasn't your fault, right? Our bodies, they fuck up."

Cheryl's expression had softened as she said, "Honey, I know."

Anna Nunez, head trainer for the Sonics, steps out of the X-ray room into the hall. She's stocky in her knee-length basketball shorts, defensive in her posture. She pauses long enough to narrow her eyes at Ruth, ignoring the other reporters entirely. "You're not getting a quote," she says. Ruth smiles and nods and, through the door Anna left ajar, spots Robbie Green, president of basketball ops. Ruth knows Robbie. She calls him when she needs a message passed to a Sonic—an apology or a clarification or a promise. When speed dial was a thing, she had his number on it.

Now he's standing against the wall opposite the X-ray machines, checking his phone. Ruth averts her gaze and silently counts to three. When she looks up again, she locks eyes with Robbie as if by chance. She enlarges hers, a solemn plea. As Robbie approaches he slides a finger down either side of his mouth, stroking the borders of his goatee. Gripping the doorframe, he leans close to Ruth.

"Open fracture, both bones," he whispers. "Turner's having surgery tonight. He'll need a rod inserted. No official prognosis yet, but this is it for him."

Ruth shakes Robbie's hand. Trusting Alison and Roxanne to take care of themselves, she runs back to the court, heels clacking on the concrete floor. She's horrified by the injury and devastated for Emory—she'll spend the remainder of the game bracing herself for another fall, the way a driver convinces herself a second car crash will follow the first—and yet there's a thrill in breaking the news. There always is. As she nears the court, she tells Phillip she's ready with an update.

"How much time do you need?" he asks.

"A minute."

Sixty seconds is long, much longer than a sideline reporter would typically speak midquarter, but Phillip doesn't argue.

"You want a camera on you?"

"Your call," Ruth says.

"Meet Julian in the tunnel."

She finds Julian at the base of the stands, cyclopsed by his hulking camera. A low railing separates Ruth from section 103. Someone sees her, and Ruth's name ripples through the rows, first as a murmur and then as a scream. A woman reaches through the metal rungs to tap her shoulder; someone else strokes the blond ends of her hair. It gets to her, the sheer quantity of people who see and touch her on a given night. Hands on her back, arms wrapped around her shoulders, lips brushing against her cheeks. Sometimes she feels the endless touching will erode her exterior, leaving her smooth and defenseless.

What Ruth misses most about marriage is knowing exactly where and with whom she belonged. Back then, days ended with her kneeled beside the bathtub, feet going numb against the floor tiles as she massaged tear-free shampoo into Ariana's scalp. Often Ruth could not believe how tired she was, how easily she could have rested her head against the enamel edge of the tub and fallen asleep. The amount of work that remained—the pajama wrestling match, the power struggle of story time, Ariana's repeated screams for water interrupting Ruth while she tried to load the dishwasher and wipe down the counters and pick up the toys and call—call *who?* Call *someone*—was staggering. Still, there was no doubt she was where she needed to be, doing what needed to be done. When she was finished she would fold up her body and tuck it against Lester's. For a minute or two, they would not speak of the child, relishing the chance to forget she existed. Then one of them would remember something cute Ariana had said that day. They would laugh. Finally they would watch the game. Because there was always a game. Even during the off-season they watched baseball or the US Open, craving hotdogs and childhood and, by the seventh inning or third set, each other.

Without flinching, Ruth faces the red light, calm and resolute. Julian cues her.

"I've just spoken with a Sonics staff member and can report that Emory Turner has suffered an open tibia-fibula fracture, meaning he has broken both bones in his lower leg. He'll need immediate surgery, and while it's impossible to say when he'll return to the court, this type of fracture takes a long time to heal. It's clear that tonight was Emory's last of the postseason—and what a year it's been for this astoundingly talented young man. Averaging twenty-six points per regular season game, thirty-two in the playoffs, Turner is unstoppable on the offensive end of the court; defensively, he's still the most impactful player on the team. Mentally we've seen him struggle in this series. Like many of us he was blindsided by Cincinnati's offense peaking at the right time, and certainly he did not expect to be competing against his former teammate and closest friend in the league, Darius Lake. But I have sat down with Emory prior to every game, have watched him cultivate both the mental toughness and humility needed to push through. This is not how any of us wanted Emory Turner's season to end—it's a devastating, shocking injury to happen during the NBA finals—but he has a lot to be proud of and we are all rooting for his full recovery."

A subtle intake of air. On the exhale: "Lester."

Her ex-husband takes over the broadcast. Ruth's arm drops to her side. She suppresses an impulse to verify that her numbers were correct; she knows they were.

Sometimes the team who has lost a player to injury is invigorated by the shock. Powered by adrenaline or determined to honor the wounded, they rally and win. Ruth has seen it happen a hundred times.

Tonight it does not happen. Kasey Powell—who, in the seconds after Emory's fall, beheld his teammate's exposed bone and vomited into a towel—misses every shot he takes. The Wildcats play with a rote but skilled efficiency, and in the final twelve seconds it's Darius who's tasked with running down the clock. In tomorrow's papers his expression will be described as inscrutable and emotionless and blank.

No one will claim it was otherwise.

CHAPTER SEVENTEEN

Ruth showers. She rinses the arena's filth from her skin, the layers of makeup from her face. Her younger self would scorn the makeup. To that well-rested, judgmental version of herself Ruth would never confess the Botox she paid a doctor to inject into her forehead a week before the playoffs. She told Joel. He laughed at her for the twenty-four hours during which she could not raise her eyebrows, no matter how surprised, sympathetic, or skeptical she became. He promised not to tell Ariana, though Ariana had taken one look at her mother over FaceTime and known. Of course she had. Ruth is worried now that whatever they shot into her face lingers in her system and is hurting the baby.

Shit. The baby.

Stepping out of the shower, Ruth retrieves her underwear from the floor, sniffs and pokes at the crotch. The material is black, impervious to stains. She runs the underwear under the faucet. The water passing through the cotton is clear. No blood then. No miscarriage.

A doctor would declare her six weeks along, meaning it

happened a month ago. Round one of the playoffs. After Cincinnati's Game Four win against the Nets (a sweep, though Brooklyn
put up a good fight) Joel appeared in Ruth's hotel room. The trip
was part business; he was interested in opening a Juniper in Clin-
ton Hill, but they made time. Her IUD had been out for months,
their condom use sporadic and dependent on Ruth's mental calcu-
lations. The math had suggested risk, but Ruth hadn't felt fertile.
It hadn't been like Ariana's conception (location: her in-laws' guest
room) when guiding Lester into her body had been as easy as folding her own hands, crossing her own legs. But after a game that
went into double overtime Ruth was exhausted, dehydrated. Still
hearing buzzers in her head. Maybe she hadn't noticed her body's
slick, spongy hospitality.

Wrapped in a towel, perched on the edge of the California
king size bed, Ruth calls Joel. He answers on the first ring. Ruth
is quiet, listening to the faint, regulatory buzz of her hotel room.
Water drips from her hair and slips down her clavicle. She's waiting to hear how much he knows. Available to him, to anyone who
cares, is the footage of Emory Turner's bone snapping; the authority with which Ruth silenced the dissenting fans, the drunkest of
whom were later escorted from the arena by security. If he's seen
it, and if he understands her at all, Joel will refrain from bringing
up the article he sent her.

She has pushed it from her mind, but the fact remains: She
promised Joel she wouldn't go after Lester's job. The weekend
before Ruth left home for Game One, she and Ariana and Joel
were making lasagna in the kitchen while a sports news program
murmured in the other room. With their fists full of grated cheese,
Ruth and Ari both froze when they heard the anchor say "Lester
Devon" and "final season in the booth."

"Did you know?" Ruth asked Ariana.

"No, I swear."

"Was he planning on telling us?" Ruth was stunned, her mouth incapable of closing.

Ariana shrugged.

"This is huge. People are going to fight tooth and nail for that job!"

Ariana smirked at her. "*Oh*. You want his games."

"No," Joel protested, clutching a bowl of spinach. "You're not serious."

Ruth gave him a look, meaning *let's talk about this later*, but he kept on discouraging her, bemoaning their shortage of hours together. He tried to recruit Ariana for his team, cajoling her, "Don't you want your mom home more often? So you guys can eat dinner together and watch *British Bake Off* and do those creepy face masks?" (Ariana, familiar with the inflexibility of her mother's aspirations, only raised her hands in surrender.) Ruth lied to Joel then because the lie pleased him and would be inconsequential once she was officially passed over for the job. The lie was also a bargain with the universe: turning the job into a double-edged sword felt like the surest way to get it.

In general, Joel has an appetite for leisure that runs counter to Ruth's need to stay in motion. He dreams of an early retirement. He delegates his responsibilities whenever possible, takes vacation often. On a trip to Hawaii, Ruth returned from an early morning run to find Joel sprawled in the sand outside their hotel, deeply asleep and wrapped in the snow-white comforter from their room. Ruth stood over him in awe: Joel had truly disconnected. From his emails, from his to-do list, from the rules governing even his own industry. (Who has ever dared to take the linens from the room?)

Ruth suspects she should envy his capacity for relaxation—but she doesn't.

Now, listening to Joel breathe into the phone, a desperate anger expands in Ruth's throat. Her jaw aches. Why does she feel, in this moment, as if history is repeating itself? Joel's stubborn silence seems to demand an apology she vowed years ago to stop making.

"Why would you send me that link?" Ruth asks finally, her voice catching on the suggestion of a sob.

Taken aback, Joel is contrite. "I'm sorry, babe. I wasn't trying to upset you. I was just confused."

"About Bell replacing Lester in the booth?"

"No. About the possibility of *you* replacing Lester in the booth. I thought we agreed that was off the table. But apparently it's a *long-anticipated* outcome for fans of Ruth Devon?"

Ruth says nothing.

"As your number one fan, I guess I'm just wondering, what the heck?"

"I'm not going to get the job," she says. "Not with Bell in the running."

"But you're up for it."

"Yes."

"Why would you hide that from me?"

Because you asked me to, she wants to say. "It's not an easy thing to navigate, this resentment you have for my job."

"I resent your absence."

"You travel pretty frequently yourself."

"Chasing you around half the time, sure. Nowhere near as frequently as you do. I actually unpack my suitcase. It has a spot on the top shelf of my closet. It's shoved up there with an old record player and a tennis racket I've never used. It's kind of awkward to grab—the racket always comes tumbling down with it. Where do you put your suitcase when you're not using it?"

Ruth's eyes close. In the middle of her bedroom floor is the answer.

Joel takes a breath. "It's not really a relationship, what we have. I want to marry you, but if you get that offer, what does that even look like?" His tone softens as he edges closer to confrontation.

"A lot like what we're doing now, I guess."

"Hotel room sex? Falling asleep with our phones pressed to our ears?"

"Yes," Ruth says.

"I want more than that."

What he wants is to marry a girl in a white dress. To send out a holiday card. He has never done these things before. Ruth supposes it would be possible to date a man six years younger than herself without feeling each of those years. But if anything, Joel has always struck her as weirdly youthful. His innocence affords him a commitment to the present moment: any meal, any film, any night (any woman?) might be the best of his life. To their relationship he brings an open-hearted enthusiasm that charms her, even as his faith that his life will grant him what he wants exhausts her. For Joel, the world still shines with a smooth layer of polish. Ruth worries she will be the one to scrub it off.

"I understand," she says. "I do too."

"You do?"

Because there are so many things she wants in addition to her work—even as she suspects she would die for her work—she says, "Of course."

Joel exhales conclusively, though no conclusion has been reached. "I'm sorry about the text. Bad timing. I wasn't thinking. How was your night?"

"Intense," Ruth says. "Awful, actually. Emory Turner broke his leg. He'll miss next season."

"Ouch. Occupational hazard, I guess."

Talking to Joel about basketball is never satisfying. She ought to avoid it.

"Speaking of injuries," Joel says, and he launches into a story. This morning, Joel and his sister took Mira to the Point Reyes lighthouse. Mira spent most of the hike in an elaborate toddler chariot hitched to Joel's back. Toward the end, she wanted to get down and walk the concrete steps descending to the lighthouse, to the rocky tip of the cape.

"She's getting pretty good at stairs, and Steph was holding her hand so we thought she'd be fine. But halfway there Mira got overly confident and shouted, 'I go down *alone!*' She yanked free of Steph's hand and immediately went tumbling, head over heels, down at least ten, maybe fifteen stairs. I'm telling you, it was terrifying."

Mira lay silent on the cement steps, chubby limbs akimbo, eyes squeezed tight against the brightness of the clouds. Joel rushed to her side, but his sister got there first. With fearful efficiency, Steph scooped the baby into her arms and gasped, "Are you okay?"

Mira exploded with laughter. "Are you okay?" she echoed, gleefully mocking her mother's panic. "Are you *okay?*"

For Ruth, this is the perfect bedtime story. Better than scrolling Twitter, as effective as Ambien; having slid beneath the covers, Ruth feels her consciousness burrowing toward sleep.

True, Joel hates basketball. True, when they go out for drinks he makes her sit with her back to the mounted TV, lest he lose her to the game. His disinterest stings, but it also protects her. Joel's affection is a respite from the noise of her industry, from the relentlessness of her own wanting. She could survive these nights without the lullaby of his voice. She could live without the furlough of their romance—but she would rather not.

He doesn't want to sacrifice sleep, Ruth reminds herself. Or to wrestle with winter coats and stroller straps and car seat buckles. He's a thirty-six-year-old man with no interest in rebuilding himself, training patience and invulnerability to nerve-fraying screams, swift sneaker kicks to the teeth. For the first sixteen months, Ruth was there, she remembers: you cultivate a mental dial tone. You coach yourself through a long game. You smell the just-soaped skin between your daughter's ear and the nape of her neck. You rest your head on hers as Max abandons the wild things and returns home to find his supper still hot, though years have passed.

Ruth says, "I'm glad Mira wasn't hurt."

"She's resilient," Joel says.

It's a cliché but also a revelation: kids are mostly okay, whether you catch them or don't. Whether you unpack your suitcase or leave on the next flight. And in this moment, the six years between Ruth and Joel are everything; she understands him better than he understands himself.

He won't mind all the buckles. Sleep deprivation will bring out his worst—but his worst won't be that bad, and after a midmorning nap and a pot of strong coffee he and his wife will laugh off their hokey, late-night hatred of each other.

Joel does want children. He doesn't want them with Ruth.

GAME FIVE

Seattle, Washington

WILDCATS – SUPERSONICS

3-1

CHAPTER EIGHTEEN

It's not the first time Ruth has seen a benchwarmer come alive in the finals. It is the first time she's witnessed Supersonic Peter Cheng make plays in transition. Or pull up above the break for a three. Certainly she's never seen him get to the rim, evading all seven feet of Anthony Moore with a lefty finger-roll. Did he just smack the floor on defense? Was that a one-legged fadeaway?

Ruth hits the talk-back button and demands of the production truck, "*What* is happening?" Phillip replies: "Girl, we are hashtag blessed."

A minute remains in the first quarter, and Cheng—a twenty-four-year-old kid two years out of Purdue—has dropped eleven points. In Ruth's ear Lester is shouting, "Did Peter Cheng just lock up Darius Lake?" while Jay repeats, "Wow wow wow," like a child's toy malfunctioning. Ruth is scribbling notes without taking her eyes off Cheng, whose slight frame hasn't prevented him from going scorched earth on the Wildcats tonight. A sweatband pushes his hair into mischievous spikes. A Band-Aid flaps from his chin. His tongue, which he sticks out after every shot, is an amphibious Powerade blue.

When Emory Turner went down in Game Four, a Game Five closeout was, in Ruth's mind, guaranteed. The Sonics can't win without Turner, not even on their home court. She forgot to account for this phenomenon: the overlooked bench player with nothing to lose unleashing the talent that got him a contract in the first place. But here it is, plunging both teams into the white-hot confusion of a fever dream. Can you even buy a Cheng jersey in the team store? Ruth doesn't know. A man seated behind the scorer's table has, on the reverse side of a homemade poster wishing Emory Turner well, scrawled BE THE CHENG.

Ruth has reason to root for a Seattle victory tonight. If Cincinnati wins, Ruth will preside, mic in hand, over the trophy presentation. She's done it six years in a row and her preference is for the champions to close it out at home. With the confetti raining down from the rafters, clinging to her glasses and her hair. With the arena's own employees embracing in the tunnel. The presentation is less daunting when the fans aren't grumbling, prematurely shuffling toward the parking lot. She wants them euphoric, their blistered screams buoying her as she ascends the stage assembled at center court and delivers the trophy to men who are, yes, happier than on their wedding days, children's birthdays, new Ferrari days. Technically, Ruth is prepared. Since Game Four she has met with her producers, with Wildcats officials and Seattle Center staff. She has memorized the list of people with whom she must speak in the immediate aftermath of a Cincinnati win. Phillip will be in her ear, guiding her, soothing her, the whole time.

Still, she would rather not.

Her preference is shameful. Ruth should want to fly home to DC and call her boyfriend from the rumpled sheets of her own bed. Then to make an appointment with her gynecologist of ten years, a woman who expressed no reservations at the removal of Ruth's IUD. Above all else Ruth should want to be in the front row at Ariana's graduation ceremony—because it matters to Ariana. Ruth herself matters enough to Ariana that she's compelled to invoke pomp and circumstance as a way of saying: *come home.* After six weeks on the road Ruth should want, should *long*, to go home.

Ruth wants Peter Cheng to hit another shot.

She wants to put her arm around him during a walkout interview and ask, on national television, "How's your night been?"

She wants to remember the kid's blue tongue, Darius Lake scratching his cheek and—see, he's not invulnerable to the magic, the miracle—smirking in disbelief.

She wants two more games.

🎙

The media will say that, prior to the fourth quarter, Cincinnati was preserving their strength. In hindsight, Peter Cheng's explosion will seem like a juvenile outburst kindly indulged by the benevolent Darius Lake—Darius, who one year ago was traded on a whim, dismissed by a Sonics franchise desperate for a championship.

Sorry, Seattle. Ninety seconds left, and Cincinnati enjoys a nine-point cushion. Darius has either scored or assisted on every Wildcats basket of the fourth quarter. On the final possession, the Sonics back off. Darius drops the ball and lets it roll across the court as his teammates mob him with their arms flung wide.

Jay, relishing his annual responsibility: "That's it! It's over! The Cincinnati Wildcats have won the championship!" He bellows the last syllable of each sentence, choo-chooing like a train pulling into the station.

Lester, mildly: "That was fun."

A pause while Jay wheezes.

Lester: "I like basketball."

The buzzer has silenced the crowd, though a smattering of displaced Cincinnati fans scream continuously, incongruously, as if celebrating a funeral. More conspicuous is the engine-purr of excuses, regrets, threats: "If only . . ." and "If Emory . . ." and "Next year, motherfuckers." Ruth's nervous system is in crisis but her legs are in charge; she rises, she steps onto the court. Though Ruth aches for Emory she believes the Wildcats deserve this win, and as she pivots from one interview to the next, absorbing collisions and hip-checks, ducking from errant elbows and expertly avoiding the camera cords snaking around her ankles, she does the players the courtesy of not asking about Turner's injury—though most of them take a second to express regrets and wish him well. She fires off fifteen questions in ten minutes. She stutters twice and watches drops of saliva fly from her tongue and land on the mic. Over and over she's aware of almost falling; but these same waves could pummel her on a hundred different courts, and no matter the series or matchup or outcome, Ruth would not go under. It means too much to her to stay afloat.

No confetti. No streamers. No house music with a bass line you can feel in your fingertips. The jumbotron looming over the court displays a feed of the US Bank Arena in Cincinnati, which is packed with fans who couldn't be here but wanted to be together. Thinking of the Ohioans who filed in by the thousands to watch their home team win on a screen nearly causes Ruth to tear up—but there's no time. The stage has been assembled. Ruth climbs the steps. In her ear, Phillip says, "If you can hear me, touch the back of your head."

Her mic is already open; even a sigh would be audible to the entire bowl. Ruth reaches up and pats her hair, which Angie has teased into her signature waves.

"Good," Phillip says. "It's time."

As always, the physical symptoms of Ruth's fear vanish the moment she hears her voice surreally projected across the stadium. First she introduces the commissioner, an underweight white man in his fifties, bald and rigid and, for no reason other than tradition, consistently booed whenever fans see his face. It's the commissioner who places the trophy in the hands of the team owner, a protocol Ruth resents. She asks the team owner—loose-lipped, bug-eyed, flushed with the kind of power available for purchase—how he feels. (He feels fantastic.) With obvious reluctance the owner transfers the trophy to Darius Lake, and Ruth can't resist commenting: "The trophy has found its rightful home."

While Darius gazes at the trophy with controlled satisfaction, his teammates lean in to kiss the globe of it, hoisting their children high enough to grab the handles of it, and Ruth interviews Rick Bellantoni.

She puts a hand on his back, not hating him. Maybe it's her reverence for the game, her devout belief that tonight is bigger than broadcasting and means more than her own ambition. Or maybe Ruth is cognizant of her power: These are the final moments of Bell's career as an NBA coach, and Ruth holds the microphone. In this moment she loves him but doesn't trust him, not for a second.

"For you, tonight concludes a long and illustrious career. Did you ever allow yourself to imagine it would end on this stage?"

"Yes," he says, teetering between flippant and overwrought.

"I think I speak for a lot of people when I say I admire your brevity. But go ahead and take as many words as you need to congratulate your team."

"Back in Cincy, during Game Four, I told them they had time. That they needed to win. I can't repeat my exact words but suffice it to say, I was not gentle." Bell looks at Ruth over the microphone. "Were you there?"

"In the locker room? Yes, sir."

"You're always there. So you know I'm no good at pep talks. Inspirational speeches are not my jam. And I don't hold hands or stroke egos. These guys have themselves to thank for this championship. They worked their asses off and they deserve it."

Next she beckons the commissioner back to present the finals MVP award. It's Darius—who else?—and he indulges in a subdued thus painfully awkward victory dance as he relieves himself of one trophy to accept another. Ruth pulls him close and steers him to the mic. She begins, "At the start of the season, no one expected this team to advance through the ranks of the playoffs, let alone win the championship. When did you first believe you had a chance?"

"Ohio was a fresh start for me. Right away I was playing more minutes and getting more touches than I was used to. Coach's confidence in me unlocked elements of my game I couldn't really access before. And the roster was already so good, and uh . . ." Darius pushes sweat from his forehead toward the grooves between his braids. "What was the question?" His laughter is deep and mechanical, rolling across the arena like the first rumbles of a storm.

Ruth tightens her arm around his back. "When did you first start to think maybe you'd get a ring?"

"Oh." Darius goes slack. "January."

Ruth maintains a straight face. "January."

Darius nods, eyelids at half-mast. "January."

Finally, Ruth invokes Emory Turner laid up in a Manhattan hospital bed, watching, she hopes, surrounded by his family.

"What do you want to say to your man Emory?" The question is casual, intimate, and based on the assumption that Darius wants to say anything at all; it's everything a question should not be.

In living rooms across the country, women flop beside their boyfriends on the couch, stealing beers and taking entitled swigs. "Who's that?" the women ask.

Low, authoritative voice booming in the arena. Tucked against the body of an athlete, undaunted by the man's size, his sweat, his valor or his vulnerability. Thick-framed glasses, red lipstick, good hair day.

"That's Ruth," the boyfriends say.

The girlfriends will frown, borderline disturbed by their boyfriends' smooth acceptance of this woman, who's not young and not old. Not a total babe but not unappealing either.

"Who is she?" they repeat.

"She's a sideline reporter," the men explain. "But sometimes she calls the games. Next year she might call the games full time."

The women infer that to call the games is to be the disembodied voice of basketball, the human layer of sound atop the whistles and squeaks and cheering. At first they can't imagine this voice as female, but after watching Ruth interview the basketball player whose dour face has been all over commercials and billboards and Twitter for weeks, they can. How Ruth will impose order and intelligence on the game, her voice a hand-clap of gentle authority warning fans to focus: Ruth Devon is in the booth and she's about to tell you something you never knew about basketball.

"Has there ever been a female announcer?" the women want to know.

The men are fairly sure they're right when they say, "No, just Ruth."

No one can tell that Ruth feels queasy. Or that the white pant-suit poses a risk that occurred to her too late: should blood bloom, it will publicize an uncharacteristic lack of foresight, revealing her as frazzled by her own fertility, distracted by daughters and boyfriends and ex-husbands and trolls. As Ruth smiles, the camera zooms and throws the creased skin beneath her eyes into high definition. She needs one more answer before she can surrender her mic for the season and climb down from the stage.

Whether or not she gets the job, she knows she's earned it. The knowledge by itself is not satisfying; when the offer is made to Rick Bellantoni or a retired player, she will shut herself into the bathroom of the master suite where she has slept alone more years than she was married and sob with her back against the shower tiles. Still, nobody can take this from her, the way Darius Lake stoops and gifts her with the first authentic grin of his career to date: in it, Ruth can see the boy on Christmas morning unwrapping the first pair of Jordans or the ball emblazoned with the official NBA logo, turning to fix his mom with this same liquefying smile. Ruth has spent half her adult life in an airport. She never got to plant a garden or adopt a dog or bust her daughter out of school for an impromptu lunch date. She got this.

Darius says, "Emory, my brother, I know you and Sasha and the girls are watching right now. I'm so grateful to you. For every-thing we've been through together. I'll see you tomorrow."

"Thank you, Darius," Ruth says, squeezing him tight before stepping aside.

"Thanks, Ruth."

CHAPTER NINETEEN

I know I've been critical of RD this season but I . . . I take it all back. She gets us emotional Darius Lake . . . and emotional Darius Lake is *chef's kiss*

Lol, Ruth Devon killing the trophy presentation and then almost falling off the stage on her way down is #relatable.

Can we get a bigger stage next year? Ruth almost went overboard!

Maybe if she wasn't wearing such high heels . . .

If she wasn't wearing such high heels she wouldn't be able to reach the players.

Did anyone else see Rick Bellantoni grab her elbow to steady her?

Yes, love that they're friends after everything.

Ruth is serving us LOOKS with that white pantsuit. Can we put this girl in the fuckin' booth already?

The hall is congested with group hugs and family photos. Camera operators stand in Ruth's way, outfitting their equipment in transparent drugstore ponchos. Pressed against an Emory Turner mural, a trio of team owners are eating chocolate-covered popcorn from a metal tin, sipping bourbon from plastic cups. Ruth elbows through the throng, turning to bestow hugs and high fives on request. Outside the locker room a set of arms wraps around her without asking permission; these arms her body knows, and for a moment of reprieve she buries her face in his dry-cleaned suit jacket.

"Call me tonight." As always his voice is in her ear, but now she can feel the moist heat of his breath, his heart beating beneath her palm.

"Why?" she shouts.

Lester whispers, "Because it's all over now—and you get so sad when it's all over."

"It's not over yet. I'm going in there!" She's in denial, hollering like a sorority sister. Her nausea has vanished. She is no longer prone to thoughts in the first-person plural.

When did the thoughts stop?

"You need a raincoat!" Lester yells at Ruth, who has already been absorbed by the scrum of reporters moving through the door.

She leaves Lester behind, screaming a promise to sit with him at the press conference.

Beneath the fluorescent lights and speckled ceiling tiles of the away team's locker room, sheets of plastic cover every surface. Interns pass out bottles of Veuve Clicquot to players festooned in championship hats and T-shirts, yellow-rimmed scuba masks to protect their eyes. As Darius dips his head toward a sea of outstretched microphones, his long fingers untwist the metal tie from a bottleneck. "I feel good," he says in placid response to a generic question. "I feel like a champion. I feel the way I like to feel."

The violence with which he shakes the bottle makes Ruth duck in self-preservation. The cork pops and soars and smacks against the ceiling. Darius covers the lip of the bottle with his thumb, spraying champagne at his teammates with volcanic force. Droplets spangle camera lenses; the footage will resemble a news report on a natural disaster. Pouring champagne into his open mouth, letting the excess cascade down his neck and soak the front of his T-shirt, Darius wails with experimental glee. His team backs him up, their volume uninhibited, their triumph the project of their young lives.

Sixth-man Florent Bandolo throws an arm around Ruth's shoulders. (Brought up to be a Catholic priest, basketball was his rebellion. Ruth can relate.) He offers her a can of Budweiser and—guiltily, giddily—she takes a gulp. She asks him, "Where y'all headed tonight?"

When inspired, Ruth can whip out a flawless y'all. She's from Virginia.

"Vegas. Can you believe I've never been?"

"It's an experience," she says. Together they watch Denzel Kerr shower Coach Morris in champagne. Andre is known for being the best-dressed coach in the NBA, and it's with debauched satisfaction that Denzel ruins the man's slim-fit suit, mock turtleneck, and thousand-dollar shoes. A PR director sticks his head into the room, summoning Darius, Denzel, and Tobin to a media room down the hall. The locker room empties as nearly everyone opts to follow the stars to the press conference. Stepping over a pile of empty bottles and dented cans, skirting frothy puddles contained by plastic sheets, Ruth moves with the flow of traffic. Her mood almost wanes but she doesn't let it. In the front row, Lester has saved her a seat.

"You're damp," he tells her.

"Champagne hurricane," she explains.

"Are you sad about Turner?"

Suspicious, Ruth puts some space between their shoulders. "What do you mean?"

"You were hoping Seattle would win. Admit it."

"I was invested in the series. I don't root."

"Please—you think I can't tell who you're rooting for?"

In short? No, she does not.

Truth is, Ruth knew it was all wrong. Emory was falling rather than landing—having lost control of his limbs, he was deadweight dropped from a second-story window. She heard the snap, she saw the heap of his body, and even before Lester used his announcer's license to declare the leg broken, Ruth knew. She wanted to be wrong. These injuries happen so fast that for a moment afterward it feels reasonable to assume they can unhappen. When it had happened to her, Ruth felt no pain initially, only the urgency of reversing the clock—*take it back, take it back*—followed by the hot seep of panic. Ruth hadn't known the layup would be her last. She had no idea a second ambition would ever succeed her first; she had felt herself permanently defeated, in pieces on the court.

Emory has a chance at a full recovery. Players have returned from compound fractures. Ruth hurts for him and wishes him peace of mind. But make no mistake: she is rooting for herself.

Darius is up on the dais, his T-shirt sopping, his goggles now strapped around his forehead and pushing against the brim of his yellow cap. Despite being soaked in alcohol and looking like a flamboyant fighter pilot, he answers questions in his usual monotone, scratching his nose and pulling on his earlobes as he speaks. A reporter from the *Seattle Times* is the first to comment on the brief but unforgettable combustion of Peter Cheng (an event that feels somehow like it transpired years ago). "Early in the second quarter the Sonics went on a seven-point run," the woman says. She has a Joan Jett haircut, reading glasses on a chain around her neck. "For a moment it seemed like you had lost control of the game—and your confidence, it wavered. Can you take us back to those minutes and explain what happened?"

"What happened?" Darius echoes.

It's a weird question, Ruth thinks. It's a question for a regular season game, or a question for the losing team. Why return to a discouraging moment? The writer must be angling for a specific response, trying to coax Darius into saying something dismissive about Cheng.

"I don't know if I remember exactly what happened. My mind is all over the place right now." And yet he chooses his words so carefully, like a man whose mind is grounded. Darius scans the rows of reporters. "RD would know." He looks at her. "Ruth, you remember anything about the Sonics going on a seven-point run?"

Ruth should not have drunk half of Florent Bandolo's beer. Because when Darius says, "Get up here," beckoning her with a curl of his fingers, she goes willingly.

"Okay." She slides into place behind a second mic. Among the camera flashes and the young men in their gingham dress shirts and sticky hairdos, she locates Phillip leaning against the back wall. His stance is wide, arms crossed. Ruth sustains eye contact with her producer, not to make a point, she doesn't think, but rather to steady herself. "With the first possession of the second quarter, Cats ran Sonics down to three on the shot clock. Kasey Powell missed a jump shot. Peter Cheng grabbed the rebound, got a dunk. Cincy came back down, ran a set for Darius"—she side-eyes him—"but you missed it, unfortunately."

He shrugs.

"Cheng got the rebound. You stopped him on the defensive end but pushed it out of bounds. The ref took it on the sideline. Powell got the ball, threw it to Cheng in the corner, step-back three. Swish. Back down the court and Cincy missed another shot. Cheng got it, went ninety-three feet, shocked us all with a pretty euro step and made a right-hand layup. Seven points. Blue tongue. Time out."

She exhales.

There's silence before the laughter, which simmers, warm and celebratory. Folding chairs groan as people shift to get a better view of the MVP smacking Ruth on the back. In the last row, his face the manifestation of hashtag blessed, Phillip brings his hands together in a slow clap. His applause is a joke, sure, but it's a joke Ruth is in on.

Her nausea returns. In protest of the beer, or her joy.

Lester was right. She gets so sad when it's all over.

In the depths of Ruth's backpack is a pregnancy test. She bought it last night, or maybe two nights ago. Before calling a cab to take her back to the Juniper, Ruth retreats to the same deserted dressing room where Angie did her hair and makeup hours earlier. She locks herself inside a stall and tears open the box. The packaging is pink and cumbersome. Paranoia prevents her from throwing it away; instead, she flattens the box and buries it in the debris of her bag, beneath the water bottles and battered notebooks and protein bar wrappers. Peeing on the stick is not a problem; she has needed to pee all night. No stage fright there. As she watches her urine seep across the plastic windowpane, her heart climbs toward her throat. A negative result, she knows, will leave her hollow and stunned. Not for conventional reasons but because knowing her own body is integral to Ruth's sense of herself. A negative result will suggest that the wires of her intuition have gotten crossed.

The first line darkens immediately, then the second catches up. Her pulse races before it slows.

All her life she has wanted babies. Staring at the positive test, the vibrations of the arena's ancient plumbing palpable beneath her feet, Ruth imagines her belly huge and taut, her whole body warm and abuzz with extra blood. She imagines the newborn's mouth on her breast, that electric twinge. She imagines her youth protracted, the thrill of newness, a brand-new person who could be anyone, rendering Ruth unfinished too. And then the fantasy cuts out.

Did the wires get crossed, or did they snap? Has she been poisoned by underground air and too much acrid coffee from the caterer's thermos? By asbestos in hotel ceilings? The radiation of airport security?

All her life she wanted babies.

She takes a picture of the test with her phone, compelled to send it to someone for instant acknowledgment. Concern or congratulations.

Her thumb hovers over the screen for a long time before she sends the picture to Lester.

CHAPTER TWENTY

In another three years, Ruth will be invited onto *60 Minutes* to be interviewed by a journalist more famous than herself. The segment will open with shots of Ruth in the booth—iconic headset framing her face, lips moving fast—before cutting to Ruth and the journalist sitting opposite each other, both women the age people are compelled to describe as "older," meaning slightly younger than "old." With studio lights vanquishing every shadow on her face, fresh blond highlights, and a new pair of glasses, Ruth will look luminous.

Cut to Ruth in a pencil skirt dribbling a basketball behind her back.

The journalist, narrating: If you've tuned into a basketball game in the last decade, then you might recognize the sound of Ruth Devon's voice. *Cut to Ruth huddled in the tunnel with her crew before a game.* With more than twenty years of experience in sports broadcasting, Devon is the first woman to call NBA games on national television. Her extensive knowledge of basketball, unparalleled composure, and ability to connect with her subjects has earned her the respect of sports fans, coaches, her fellow announcers and, most importantly, the players themselves. *Cut to a shot of Ruth and Emory Turner embracing at Emory's first game following his injury.* But call her a breaker of glass ceilings or a trailblazer for women in sports broadcasting, and she just might push back.

Ruth: Am I the first woman to fill this particular role? Yes. Am I the first woman to achieve a certain status in the eyes of the culture? Maybe. But listen, there were women walking into locker rooms, microphone in hand, long before me. In baseball, football, you name it. And some of those women had doors slammed in their faces. Some of them, like Patricia O'Connor with the New York Yankees, heard things like "I'm not talking until that (*bleep*) leaves the room." Nothing like that ever happened to me. I feel extremely privileged.

Journalist: Tell us about the day you got the call.

Ruth: I was—I was alone in my car. My daughter had just graduated from high school, and I was on my way to meet her and her dad—

Journalist: Retired coach and broadcaster Lester Devon.

Ruth: Right. That guy. I was on my way to meet them for dinner. Earlier, at the ceremony, Lester had intimated that I might be receiving good news by the end of the day. He was still at the network back then, so he was in the know. As you can imagine, it was already a big day for me. I was happy, but suddenly I'm on edge. I'm sitting in my car, reading on my phone about Emory Turner's injury. This was right after he broke his leg in Game Four and Seattle lost the championship.

The journalist smiles blankly.

Ruth: Everyone was talking about how the injury would affect his free-agency options. It was June, and free-agency begins in July, so there was a lot of speculation in the media. Turner had been seen dining out at some fairly upscale establishments with Darius Lake, who was at that time the star player in Cincinnati. Rumor was, Turner was thinking of signing with the Wildcats.

Ruth realizes too late that the journalist is not a basketball fan. She supposes the past minute will end up on the cutting room floor. Whatever. At least they're not live.

Ruth: Then a call comes in. It's my producer.

The journalist's lips curl into a controlled smile, designed not to wrinkle her face.

Journalist: So he offers you the job. How did you respond?

Ruth: I cried.

Cut to footage of Ruth and the journalist strolling across Ruth's freshly mown lawn in Potomac Falls. Ruth is wearing an Elena Delle Donne sweatshirt, throwing a tennis ball for her mother's dog.

Journalist: Before you were a full-time analyst, you were a sideline reporter.

Ruth: For twenty years.

Journalist: During the finals, the network still sends you back to the sideline.

Ruth: Yes, for five to seven games at the end of the post-season, I go back to the sideline.

Journalist: Is that disappointing?

Ruth: First of all, I believe I'll get my chance to call the finals if that's something I want to do. It may not be this upcoming season or the one after that, but it will happen. Secondly, the sideline reporter's job is to be there on the floor and at practice and in locker rooms connecting with players on a personal level. The sideline reporter gives fans insights they can't get from watching the game or listening to the announcers. I think the network is being honest with me when they say, "Look, it's an important job, and we don't have anyone else of your caliber to do it." Now, am I supposed to take offense? Am I supposed to sulk because I haven't quite earned the legendary status of the men in the booth on those particular nights? Those men are my colleagues. I have nothing but respect and admiration for them. It's not required of me, as a woman, to feel aggrieved or undervalued when what I feel is grateful.

Cut to footage of Ruth in her kitchen holding a cocktail and a bowl of popcorn, trying to move past her daughter who appears concerned with the arrangement of her mother's bangs.

Journalist: I want to ask you a question I probably wouldn't ask a man.

Ruth: Okay.

Journalist: Earlier in the year you were quoted in *The New Yorker* saying, "I never saw any of this coming. What I wanted was to be a stay-at-home mom."

Ruth: That's the truth.

Journalist: You have one daughter. (*Long pause.*) She's twenty-one now. (*Longer pause.*) How often were you home when she was growing up?

Ruth: In reality? About half the time. But it felt like never.

Journalist: Being a mom, staying home, packing school lunches, driving the kids to soccer practice and dance class: Are you glad you avoided it?

Ruth: Not at all. Those were the things I sacrificed! I wanted it both ways—and if I'm being completely honest with you, I still want it both ways. I would love to see how an alternate version of my life plays out, one where I stay married and have five kids and drive a big ol' SUV around the suburbs of Virginia. When I think about the siblings my daughter doesn't have, all the nights I spent in the underground of an arena instead of putting her to bed . . . It kills me to know I can't get those years back.

Journalist: You were also quoted in *The New Yorker* saying basketball is "the great love of your life."

Ruth: Yeah.

Journalist (*with Sunday night seriousness*): Was it worth it?

Ruth: You would have to ask my daughter.

CHAPTER TWENTY-ONE

Ruth gets to the football field early but not as early as Lester. As she makes her way down a grassy aisle between rows of wedding-white folding chairs, other moms watch her from the corners of their eyes; college-age brothers nudge their fathers, some of whom lift a palm and say, "Hi, Ruth." Strangers, as far as she knows. Sliding into the seat Lester has saved her, three rows back from the stage erected over the end zone, Ruth knows the two of them together is more of a spectacle than either alone. Still, Lester's is the only company into which she can recede, forgetting the onlookers entirely. She greets him with: "Think they sell popcorn at this thing?"

"No refreshments, I already checked. We're lucky they put up a tent. It's sweltering." The way Lester is fanning himself with the program makes him appear, to Ruth, adorably yet irredeemably old.

"Where's Joel?" he asks. It's new, Lester referring to Joel by his first name instead of calling him *Fernandez* or Ruth's *paramour*. It's overdue.

"His flight was delayed, landed about an hour ago. He'll be here." She rests her purse on the empty chair beside her.

Three nights ago, when Ruth returned to her hotel room after Game Five, the pregnancy test in her bag as heavy as a gun or a wad of hundred-dollar bills, Joel was waiting for her. "It's over!" he shouted, arms flung wide in celebration. He meant the NBA finals, but Ruth felt no satisfaction. She felt gutted and shortchanged, as if evacuated from the coast halfway through vacation, or dismissed from the table before dinner was over. The summer months without basketball have always felt surreal. She never fully shakes the impulse to turn on the game and check the score. The idea of teams disbanding, dispersing among hometowns and vacation hot spots, disorients her. Without the ever-building narrative of the season and the playoffs, she lives half in the past and half in prognostications about next season.

Leaning into Joel's embrace, all she could think was: *no more basketball.* What would she watch? What would she read? What would distract her from Ariana's Instagram or the cold dread of her own mortality?

The terror would subside; in another day she would reacquaint herself with her overgrown backyard and bleach-white towels and sleek, smiling daughter. She would make an appointment with her doctor and spend the ensuing hour lying across her bed with her hands on her lower abdomen, cementing the decision in her mind again and again, gut twisting, heart thudding. She didn't believe she would or would not regret it. She believed she would never know what she ought to have done—and that she could live, not knowing.

Lester puts his arm around the back of her chair. "So did you tell him?"

She shakes her head. If she gets into it, she will cry, and she would sooner let Lester see her naked than see her cry.

There's a silence before Lester says, "I have to admit, I didn't like imagining you having a kid with someone else. I've accepted that you're not my wife, but you've always been the mother of my daughter. You being the mother of some other guy's daughter? Not to be melodramatic, but huge betrayal."

Willfully, Ruth dodges Lester's point. "The baby could have been a boy."

He ignores her. "Is that how you'd have felt if I'd knocked up someone else?"

"Rumor is you got snipped."

"But what if I hadn't?"

"I would have worried that your new baby would replace your first baby. Like you'd love Ariana less, or think of her less, or look out for her less because you'd have a new child with a woman you'd, presumably, love. I would have been jealous and cagey and a little bit heartbroken for Ariana's sake, but not my own."

Lester, impressed: "You thought about this."

"Often."

"I never thought about you having another guy's kid until I caught you puking your guts out in Cincinnati."

"I know," Ruth says.

Ruth twists in her seat to see the football field filling with families. Among the mid-Atlantic grandmas in their Easter dresses, the bored little sisters and anxious moms, Joel moves down the aisle alone. He has traveled in a blue suit, a shabby leather duffel bag smacking against his left hip. Apologies drip charmingly from his lips as he turns into the third row, sidestepping between knees and chair-backs. Throwing himself beside Ruth, he smells like stress-sweat and spiced cologne.

"Sorry I'm late," he says, taking Ruth's face in his hands and kissing her. The kiss is not nonproprietary, which she appreciates and also doesn't. "You look beautiful. It's so hot here. Hi, Lester."

Lester nods at Joel. "You're moist. You're a sentient swamp."

"Thanks, man."

The school principal mounts the stage with her coiffed blond bob and black robe billowing. Audience members sink, unhurried and still chatting, into chairs. The principal asks them to please silence their phones. As Ruth gropes blindly in the depths of her purse, endeavoring to ignore the tension radiating from the men on either side of her, Lester whispers in her ear: "The moment the ceremony's over, I want you to turn your ringer back on."

His breath is warm and farm-scented. She looks at him. It's fair to say her life flashes before her eyes.

There's no denying Lester loves her. When they were married, he protected her and tended to her—icing her bad knee after workouts, paying off her credit card debt, throwing surprise parties on her birthday. After she gave birth to their daughter, he, cradling the newborn like a football, looked Ruth in the eye and said, "I can never pay you back for this. Don't let me forget."

But within a few years, Ruth had discovered her husband was incapable of rooting for her.

"With the volume on loud," Lester adds.

She feels nothing, and then she feels airborne. She would divorce him a thousand times if signing the papers guaranteed this moment. "Really?" Her voice comes out helium-high. Nostrils flaring as she struggles to keep it together: "Oh, shit."

Joel is staring straight ahead as high schoolers fill the stage.

He's the first to lift an arm and wave at Ariana, flashing her two thumbs-up and an unrestrained grin.

"Shit," Lester agrees.

After the kids have flipped their tassels and tossed their hats—all the girls running prompt, precise fingers through their hair—and Ruth has wept a little more than she planned on weeping, pride compounded by hormones and anticipation, she checks her phone.

No missed calls.

On the football field Ari breaks away from a cluster of friends and comes flying, all speed and heedlessness, at her mother. Ruth savors the collision, the uninhibited violence of it. She remembers when her daughter thrashed inside of her, and she remembers when she tore her way out, and Ruth stops feeling the way she usually does—as if she's lived several lives since then. Up close, Ruth can count Ariana's pimples, see the sunlight trapped in her halo of frizzy hair, lament the seven-thousand-dollar Invisalign the girl refuses to wear.

"You're here!" Ariana says. "And Dad's here! And I never have to go to school again!"

"We'll see," Ruth says.

Two weeks from now, a newly hollowed Ruth will accompany Ariana to a photoshoot on Ocean Avenue in Santa Monica. Expecting resistance, Ruth will be surprised when Ariana seems amused by her mother's sudden need to shadow her. Grateful, Ruth will at first hang back but soon find the environment pleasantly familiar. She will engage the photography assistant in a discussion of long-term career goals; she will confirm that the makeup artist is using a foundation with adequate sun protection. When Ariana and the photographer embrace—having worked together before, evidently—the man, with his pale, concave cheeks, Lennon glasses, and mop of graying hair, looks askance at Ruth. To Ari he says, "You're eighteen, aren't you?"

"Oh yeah," Ari answers. Her outfit is more juvenile than anything she would wear in real life: a fraying denim skirt, a sweatshirt advertising Niagara Falls in retro cursive. The skirt is too small, the sweatshirt too large. Both items look thrifted. The clothes are beside the point, Ruth supposes. The point is the model's body—a fantasy version of the consumer's. "Mom gets lonely during the off-season."

Wrinkling his forehead: "Off-season?"

Ruth and Ariana will exchange a look, silently agreeing to explain nothing.

It's the photographer on whom Ruth keeps a watchful eye. She doesn't appreciate his need to verify Ariana's age, nor his habit of objectifying his model in the third-person: "Have her put her left hand on her hip." "That smile should be more American." "Pull the sweatshirt down over the shoulder." Distracted by what she perceives as disrespect, Ruth almost overlooks the young, handsome set stylist who, an hour into the shoot, notices the Band-Aid wrapped around Ariana's right index finger.

"Hold up." Nathan is a Black twenty-two-year-old with short twists and a fashionably misshapen T-shirt. Carefully he peels the Band-Aid from Ariana's finger, stuffing it into the pocket of his skinny jeans. (How and when did Ariana hurt herself? Ruth will want to know, refrain from asking.) Ariana thanks him, the rising temperature of her cheeks perceptible, perhaps, only to her mother.

That night, Nathan will drive his burnt-orange nineties Beemer to the Airbnb Ariana is sharing with Ruth. By agreeing to go out, by wearing an unbuttoned blazer over a lace bralette, Ariana could be testing her mother: How badly do you want to be here? How much power do you think you have? The answers would be hard to articulate. Ruth would be tempted to assert there's nowhere she'd rather be. But isn't there?

As for her power, Ruth knows she has none. And maybe Ariana's decision to go to dinner with Nathan has nothing to do with Ruth. Maybe Ariana likes beautiful boys and tacos from Guisados and balmy summer nights on Sunset Boulevard.

At the door, Ruth says, "Have fun."

When Nathan says, "Thanks, Ruth," in what can't be an accidental echo of every player who has ever named her on air, Ruth is torn between laughing and rescinding her unsolicited blessing. Of the people in Ariana's life, particularly those whom Ruth did not personally select, Ruth always itches to approve or disapprove fully. Her anxiety leaves no room for nuance. Watching Ariana climb into the kid's vintage car, Ruth resists her own judgment, arbitrary as it would have to be. Ruth is likely to learn nothing of the date, and to never see Nathan again.

Waiting up all night, intermittently texting Lester about free-agency rumors, Ruth vows to study up on the jargon and standards of Ariana's industry. From now on Ruth will pore over every contract and remain alert to breaches. She will buy a small apartment in Los Angeles, a home base for the two of them on the West Coast. She will impose herself on Ariana's adulthood, prepared to be both resented and relied upon. Over the years that follow, Ruth and Ariana will form a tradition of meeting in New York during fashion week. For Ruth, the ritual becomes the perfect excuse to avoid the nauseating spectacle of All-Star Weekend, the sport she takes dead-seriously caricatured in the Celebrity Game, the Dunk Contest. Ruth will be surprised at how quickly she learns to enjoy the lustrous theater of the runway, at how easily she memorizes the names of the designers, photographers, brands, and agencies. She will stop torturing herself on Instagram. She will acknowledge the inhumanity of measuring her own failures in the exposed flesh of her daughter.

On the football field Ruth presses her nose into the top of Ari's head. She breathes in the only human smell that doesn't currently make her want to barf. Ruth is too old to be pregnant and yet she's younger than the other mothers fawning over their graduates. Briefly, Ruth wonders if she's denying Ariana a crucial gift: a person with whom she shares a mother.

A person who knows what it means to be Ruth Devon's child.

CHAPTER TWENTY-TWO

"Lester meeting us at the restaurant?" Joel asks, buckling himself into the passenger seat of Ruth's car. Ariana is riding with her father. Ruth murmurs vaguely in Joel's direction, hypnotized by the rumors on her phone. Emory Turner and Darius Lake had dinner together in New York. Emory, who has been infuriatingly opaque on the subject of free-agency. And Darius, who has proven himself a player at the peak of his powers.

Would Emory really leave Seattle for Cincinnati? Does his friendship with Darius—or a championship ring—mean that much after all?

Ruth's thoughts run wild. Turner signing with the Wildcats would be league-shaking. And what would the team look like restructured? Like a reincarnation of the Supersonics two seasons ago? Would Darius retain his present role as the focal point of the offense? Is anyone sure that Emory will recover and be the same player? Would it be worth jettisoning multiple players—as the Cats would have to do to get under the salary cap—for an Emory who's a shell of his former self?

And in the best-case scenario, in which Emory and Darius slip seamlessly back into the league's most formidable pick-and-roll partnership, *who* is going to coach this team?

The answers to these questions matter to Ruth—and not just because she's paid to obsess over the possible outcomes. If Emory signs with Cincinnati, Ruth will follow him there. She'll have to return to that dressing room, to the smells of that aging arena and to the sound, echoed in her memory, of bones breaking.

Ruth refrains from texting everyone she knows. She's getting ahead of herself. This was a dinner between best friends, nothing unusual about that. (Though, theoretically, their friendship provides the perfect cover: Emory can't take official meetings until July.) The fans' hysterical thirst is an urge she herself must not feel, even if her job is to quench it.

Her phone is ringing. Her obsession with the dinner in New York evaporates. She has pressed the phone to her ear and said "Hello?" before she has fully registered the incoming call. She ought to have taken a second to steel herself. Or cross herself. Or clear the rasp from her voice.

Ruth trusts Phillip to cut to the chase, and he does.

"RD, I'm not going to lie to you. There were a lot of discussions. Endless back-and-forth. Things got ugly when people started throwing Bell's name around. But ultimately, the execs left it up to the producers, and once they did that, well, it was an easy choice. The job is yours."

Ruth has always wondered how it would feel to get what she wants, and now she knows.

Joel has climbed out of the car. Either because he didn't hear Phillip's voice through the speaker, or because he did and would rather not hear Ruth's response. He stands in the high school parking lot with his back to the windshield, hands in his pockets. There's something hesitant in his posture, as if he can't decide whether to lean against the hood or do a lap around the lot.

Ruth is alone. Her tears are instant, silent even as they rattle her. She's only half conscious of pressing a hand against her abdomen. That peel of laughter—it's warm and poised and destined for airwaves. "I'm grateful, Phillip, but I think you're lying to me. I know how many qualified candidates were in the running. It must have been an extremely difficult decision for the network."

Phillip says, "No, Ruth. You're peerless."

ACKNOWLEDGMENTS

As always, I want to first thank my agent, Susan Ginsburg, for everything she does on my behalf. I'm also grateful to her assistant, Catherine Bradshaw, and to everyone at Writers House who supported this book.

My writing has benefited enormously from Peggy Hageman's sharp editorial skills. I was lucky enough to work with Peggy on two books, including *The Second Season*, before she died. I will miss her feedback and her friendship; I wish she'd had more time.

Thank you to everyone at Blackstone Publishing, including Lauren Maturo, Jeffrey Yamaguchi, Josie Woodbridge, Rick Bleiweiss, Naomi Hynes, Alenka Linaschke, Greg Boguslawski, Megan Wahrenbrock, Ember Hood, Hannah Ohlmann, Ciera Cox, and Mandy Earles. It has been a pleasure working with all of you.

Huge thanks to Brooke Olzendam for taking the time to talk me through a day in the life of an NBA sideline reporter; I remain a devoted fan. I'm also grateful to Geoff Butler for answering my many questions about broadcasting.

Thank you to friends and first readers: Carolyn Eyre, Kerry

Winfrey, Liz Zaretsky, and especially Lauren Rochford, who never lets me miss a Woj bomb.

Thanks to my brother Andy for modeling a lifelong NBA obsession, and to my sister-in-law Char for reading a messy first draft and cheering me on.

And thank you to Dan—because when I said, "Who's that?" you said, "That's Doris."